PREVIOUS BOOKS BY THE AUTHOR

Poetry
The Bleeding Ballerina
Moody Bitch

Short Stories
The Glass Whittler
All the Tenderness Left in the World

Novels
Crimes by Neglect
The Heart's Wild Surf
The Whistler
Belief
The Shag Incident
Music From a Distant Room

DEDICATION

For thou T.H.O.W.

drowned sprat

and other stories

Stephanie Johnson

ν
VINTAGE

ACKNOWLEDGEMENTS

'In a Language All Lips' and 'You'll Sleep with No Other' first published in *The Glass Whittler*, New Women's Press, 1988

'Taken in the Rain', 'Menschenfresser' and 'Striker Lolls' first published in *All the Tenderness Left in the World*, University of Otago, 1993

'Red Lolly' and 'The Night I Got My Tuckie' broadcast on Radio New Zealand, 2003

'Three Times A Week' and 'Box of Stones' previously published in *Metro*

'Race', 'The Night I Got My Tucki', 'Phone Gene' and 'Bali, Baby' previously published in the *New Zealand Listener*

'Mother Maryam' previously published in *Bosom Buddies*, Black Swan, 2003

'The Night I Got My Tuckie' previously published in *The Best New Zealand Fiction Volume 1*, edited by Fiona Kidman, Vintage, 2004

National Library of New Zealand Cataloguing-in-Publication Data
Johnson, Stephanie, 1961-
Drowned sprat and other stories / Stephanie Johnson.
ISBN 1-86941-678-3
I. Title
NZ823.2—dc 22

A VINTAGE BOOK
published by
Random House New Zealand
18 Poland Road, Glenfield, Auckland, New Zealand
www.randomhouse.co.nz

First published 2005
© 2005 Stephanie Johnson
The moral rights of the author have been asserted
ISBN 1 86941 678 3

Text design: Elin Termannsen
Cover design: Katy Yiakmis
Printed in Australia by Griffin Press

Contents

Bali, Baby   7
Box of Stones   17
The Night I Got My Tuckie   35
Oy Joy   44
Red Lolly   54
In a Language All Lips   60
Red Button   66
Striker Lolls   77
Race   87
My Private Joy, My Comfort   93
Menschenfresser   102
Phone Gene   111
Taken in the Rain   120
Clumsy Machine   133
The Colour of Flesh   154
Fable   161
Mother Maryam   174
Maximum Turnover   184
You'll Sleep with No Other   195
'. . . into the care of his mother'   202
Nativity with Endymion   215
Three Times a Week   222
Drowned Sprat   229

Bali, Baby

Suddenly she is surrounded by three hard-faced white girls and an older woman, all with cameras held to their eyes, a rush of them across Jalan Legian to join a crowd of ten or so others who, Sarah sees now, are all quietly pointing their cameras in the same direction. She turns to see where she is, where the family has got to on this flaming barbecue of a Bali afternoon in late September. They draw up behind her, her husband and three daughters, the youngest one reaching immediately to touch a bunch of bright fake flowers tied to the hoarding. The Sari Club.

Two women, both in crocheted bikini tops and squitty denim shorts, step closer and then from side to side, clicking, taking in a poem, a tribute, a sun-bleached toy kangaroo, a battered teddy, a row of portraits, the lists of names. Fluidly, one of them squats to snap a fallen wreath of pink and green plastic flowers, small enough to fit a child's wrist. A butterfly emerges on the skin of her shiny, tanned buttock above her shorts, framed by the pink elastic of her G-string. Her thin, rippling back is set with several black moles and above it her splintery hair is caught up with a plastic clasp on the top of her head. She is perhaps eighteen, not quite twenty, the same age Victor would have been had he lived. The girl is sun-blasted, her freckly face solemnly riveted into an expression of grief and important, patriotic trauma. Beside her, Jimmy is gaping slightly, not at the butterfly, but at the fence and the desolate square of dirt on the other side, as he draws his camera from his bag.

'Don't take photographs of it, Dad,' instructs fifteen-year-old Lily bossily, one hand on her saronged hip, a scowl deepening under the beak of her cap. 'That's gross.'

'Is this where the Bali bomb was?' Annie squints up at her mother, the sun flaring on her spectacles.

'That's right.' Why did seeing that girl bring Victor to mind? Sarah wonders. Apart from his projected age, he would have had nothing in common with her. He would have been darker. Much darker . . . but then he didn't leave her with much to remember him by — just a fading picture now, of his little face wrapped in the hospital shawl. She hardly ever thinks of him. He lived his few hours years ago, before she even met Jimmy. Before sensible Jimmy saved her from her too-often-unsensible self.

'Did all these people get killed?' Annie waves in the direction of the pictures on the fence; Lily and Margot flank their father. Maybe, observes Sarah, even though Jimmy hasn't lived in Australia for almost twenty years, he's having a moment of solidarity with his countrywomen. But the ruin chills her heart and in some way irritates her, but she doesn't have the energy to define why in this blistering heat, with Annie's overactive imagination churning in the eight-year-old skull beside her, level with her waist, shaded by a lurid orange crocheted brim. Sarah hooks an arm around her.

'Let's go,' she says, drawing Annie away.

'Why were those ladies wearing their bikinis in the street?' asks Annie in the taxi van on the way back to Sanur.

'Because they haven't learnt anything since the —' Sarah begins, but Jimmy cuts her off.

'Because the beach isn't far away. Kuta Beach.' He has a warning tone in his voice. Not too much information, says the tone — you always tell them too much. The picture you give them is too bleak.

Margot leans a skinny brown arm across her mother to slam the van window shut against the fumes.

'Skodie! Look at that poxy river,' she says, pointing at a plastic-clogged shallow canal. Her face registers real shock, her eyes wide — brilliant blue set in the purest white. Alongside the waterway, factories and workshops mar the few remaining paddy-fields, a patchwork broken into ragged squares. There are drooping shanties, skinny dogs and an old man bent over his plants. Further on, acres of mangroves thrive in the mud, a delta opening out beyond them towards the sea. Then they are at the corner with its KFC, red and white polymer walls, a monstrous carnival house, the ever-encroaching sideshow of America.

When will the Americans come back in person, wonders Sarah, if they ever do? Doleful locals had told her and Jimmy that the Americans stopped coming to Bali after September 11, long before the Kuta bomb, their departed dollar lamented by the shopkeepers and hoteliers, but otherwise, seemingly, unmourned.

'I've got a taste for chips,' announces Annie, squinting at the

KFC sign. 'I wish we could have some chips —' but the taxi van is wheeling around the intersection and winding the narrow road into Sanur.

Almost of a height, Lily and Margot lead the way into the hotel lobby, where they swim through conditioned air colder than the water of the pool will be. In their rooms they change, find their books and hurry through the compound down towards the pool by the beach restaurant. It's late afternoon and all the deck chairs and umbrellas are taken, except for one by the children's pool. A small Japanese boy stands under the gushing mouth of a concrete frog, watching Jimmy rub sun block into Sarah's back.

'Makes you realise,' says Jimmy, pushing down the straps of her togs, 'just how bad it was. Seeing that wall. We didn't get the full brunt of it at home.'

'Mmm.' Sarah doesn't want to think about it. She concentrates all her being into the skin directly under his moving hands.

'Did we?'

'Immm.' Sarah leans a little into the pressure of his fingers.

'Do you think,' says Jimmy, and she feels his warm lips, the prickle of his two-day beard, pressing into the back of her neck, 'do you think the kids'd notice if we disappeared for a while?'

Annie sits on the edge of the bigger pool, dangling her legs, her glasses still on, focusing into the depths. Margot and Lily are doing underwater handstands, competing to see who can stay down the longest. There are a few adults and other children: a fat, loud, sandy-headed Australian boy; a pale English rose with her grandparents lovingly towing her around; three micro-thonged, golden-skinned German teenagers.

'It's too hot,' says Sarah, just as Jimmy goes on: 'The girls'll look after Annie.'

'How can they? They're upside down.'

With a sigh, Jimmy registers her rebuff and returns to his own chair.

With the slap of a slipper being thrown to the floor, the tree behind them drops one of its long, flat leaves. Annie slides into the pool, leaving her glasses folded on the edge where someone is bound to stand on them. Lily comes to the surface, gasping, and Margot ceases counting out the seconds — 'One-Mississippi, Two-Mississippi' — even though their mother has tried to teach them Paremata, which has the same number of syllables and none of the allure.

As Sarah makes her way to rescue the specs a dispute erupts between the girls over Margot's time-keeping. Lily stands chest-deep, shouting, one young breast escaped from its triangle of cloth.

'Lily,' says Sarah gently, and when her daughter looks up, drops her gaze. Lily understands immediately and ties her bikini tighter with emphatic movements before heaving herself out of the water and striding over to take her mother's chair. The glasses in hand, Sarah watches Lily's mouth move — she's too far away to hear — and eventually Jimmy lies his book on his chest and closes his eyes. He could be sleeping, but Lily appears to believe he's listening and talks on.

Sarah drops down, sitting on the warm wet concrete where Annie had been, and soaks her feet in the water. A quartet of large women wallow beside her, telling one another of their various bargains: the already-in-transit-to-Sydney sets of hand-hewn garden furniture beaten down to below cost; cushion covers and curtains run up for nix. They move on to food — what they've eaten today and how bad or good it was. Sarah tunes out, borne away from her eavesdropping on a sudden wave of anger.

Greedy pigs, she wants to say to them. Look around you. Look at the poverty — spend your big fucking dollars.

The women are probably regular visitors, tourists who can hold up both hands in response to the constant question, 'You come here how many times?' When she and Jimmy are asked that question they can only shake their heads. 'Never before. First time.' It's not true, of course — not for Sarah. She was here once before, in 1983. She should hold up one finger.

'You like it?' is usually the next question and they reply, or the girls do, 'Yes, very much. Very nice.'

'Thes es just beuddiful,' sighs the woman closest, and lies back on the surface of the water, offering herself to the sun, her stomach a flowered island of beach-ball proportions.

For the next half hour, while Annie demonstrates her duck-diving prowess and Margot brings her mother floating frangipani blossoms that have fallen in the pool, Sarah castigates herself for not luxuriating, not giving in to the indulgences of a resort holiday. This is the real rest, the tonic, the reconstitution of the harried soul, the convalescence of the tired body. But sometimes, waking in the cool early dawn to the whirring of the fan, Sarah has thought she was in a hospital. There was the same knowledge that all your bodily needs would be taken care of, a mild infantilising. You bought yourself a moment's return to the nursery.

Carrying their towels, Jimmy is walking towards her.

'Come on,' he ruffles her hair. 'Lil says she'll watch them.'

He hasn't given up hope, then. And looking up at his wicked, inviting smile, Sarah feels that old warm rush for him, the gift of it.

By the time she's taken Annie's glasses over to Lily and followed the path back to their room, Jimmy is already lying back waiting for her. She goes to him quickly and takes him in her arms and the pleasure they have in each other surprises her again, as it often does — it's like a secret, something deeply unfashionable and for most people undesirable, to have the same lover for most of your life. Perfect — or at least enough for each other — graceful, swift, skilled: the irritations and distance of the afternoon dispel with every caress. They feel all of their good luck.

Why can't it be like this all the time? Sarah wonders, snuggling into him afterwards, a slick of sweat between their two skins. Why do we have to lose our way here? Years ago, when the girls were tiny, she'd realised it was like this: sex was a room they could go to if they wanted — go through the door and find the other waiting on the other side. She'd thought then that there would always be the glitter and joy and celebration of that warm room, their grateful returns to it after jags of aridity, or resentment, or ill-health.

'How long will it last?' she asks him.

'What?' Jimmy is nearly asleep, one arm thrown above his head onto the pillows, its pale underside gleaming in the late afternoon light.

'This.'

'Oh,' says Jimmy. 'Do you want first shower?'

'It won't last forever, you know,' she says. 'It stops. I think it must all come to an end. When there's no chance of any more children, even when you don't want any more, when there's no need for it.'

'For godsake.' He's getting out of bed, wrapping his damp towel around his waist. 'Why can't you just enjoy things?'

'But I did — I —'

'Accept what we've got —'

'But I did enjoy it. I —'

'I'm not talking about sex,' he says, suddenly furious. 'I mean generally. It's all right just to enjoy life, you know, to be happy, instead of waiting for the next calamity. It's a bad habit you've got, bad conditioning. You've always had it, since I met you. We've worked hard for all this.'

'Maybe it isn't a calamity, by then, by the time it stops,' Sarah murmurs, but Jimmy has closed the bathroom door after him.

Before dinner they gather the family together and go for a walk along the concrete pathway that leads along Sanur Beach, past hotels and gardens, palm trees, strings of stalls and warungs. Annie walks ahead on lolly lookout, Margot and Lily dawdle behind, Margot whistling through her teeth in a way she knows sets Lily's nerves on edge. By the time they reach the beach market they're surrounded by stall-holders, mostly smiling women, plucking at their sleeves — 'You come in my shop? You come see?' — pointing, cajoling.

'No, not now,' says Jimmy, 'Jalan jalan,' and after a while, rudely, 'Nyeri to!' One by one they drop away, all except one woman carrying a baby who stays silently by Sarah's side. It's not until they pass out the other side of the market, the massive edifice of the Grand Bali Beach Hotel looming up before them, that Sarah even realises she's there.

'You good mother,' the woman says urgently. 'One-two-three,' she counts Sarah's daughters. 'You want to buy my baby?'

Sarah stops walking and looks for the first time directly at the woman. She's not young — perhaps in her late thirties or early forties — thin, with bad teeth. But the baby is healthy, with cotton-thread bracelets around his plump wrists, his round tummy and shoulders glistening with oil. He is around ten months old.

'You want to buy my baby? You only got girls — this a boy —' the woman begins again, closer.

'No!' Sarah finds herself laughing, just once, in disbelief. 'You don't mean that. You can't want me to . . .'

Up ahead, Jimmy is pointing out the glass-bottom boat chugging through the lagoon, a tall prahu skimming on blue outriggers behind it, a painted eye on the prow. The baby smiles at Sarah, waves his fists.

'I can't,' she tells the woman, and wonders if it is in fact her baby. Is she the grandmother? 'Even if I wanted to, I couldn't take him into my country. I wouldn't be allowed to.'

The woman is staring at her and Sarah sees that the tired eyes are filling with tears.

'Sorry,' Sarah says quietly. 'He's a lovely baby.' And she pats the woman's narrow shoulder before hurrying on.

It's not until the next day that she tells Jimmy about it, while they walk through the monkey forest in Ubud.

'Did you give her anything?' he asks. Monkeys cluster around a man feeding them with what looks like sweet potato; two young females fight for a chunk of it near Lily's feet. She steps backwards, cautious.

'What?'

'Money.'

'She wasn't begging.'

'Of course she was.'

A tubby boy is teasing an adult male with a banana. Suddenly the monkey takes a flying leap and lands on the boy's shoulders, leaning over his head and grabbing with a sinewy arm at the fruit. As the boy spins, hooting and shrieking with panic, Sarah recognises him: the sandy-haired boy from the hotel pool. Around them the Balinese erupt into laughter. The boy's father, his forearms blue with tattoos, calls out, 'Give him the bloody banana, Dwayne, give him the bloody thing.'

'Maybe we could take the baby?' Sarah asks quietly. 'Maybe we could arrange it properly. Legally.'

'Of course not. Be realistic. Sit down next to that monkey on the wall.' He opens the camera case while Sarah does as she's told. The monkey pats her with its dry little black hands before trying to tug off her watch and, after a moment, frustrated by its attachment, it bites her.

There is only a little bit of blood and the rest of the family seem to find it amusing. As they walk up to the gate for the dab of disinfectant and sticking plaster Lily even makes a crack about Ebola virus.

Most evenings for the rest of their holiday they take the walk along the pathway by the sea, and although Sarah looks out for the woman and child, she never sees them again. And when the holiday is over and they've taken the plane back to New Zealand, and their tans of privilege have faded, even then, now and again, she finds herself fretting, at odd times of the day, wondering what became of the child, whether the woman succeeded in giving him away, and if the people who took him are giving him love and nourishment, or at the very least treating him kindly. She thinks of him more than she does the lost baby of her own, the son who would now be a young man and who she may have lost anyway, especially if she'd stayed in Australia to raise him, and if he'd grown up to be one of those young tourists partying in the Sari Club on that October night in 2002.

Box of Stones

Under this flat, grey sky, on an autumn day in 1980, it suddenly seemed as though he could see the hearts and minds of the girl and boy and those of their generation as clearly as he could see the stones around him, as far as the edges of Birdlings Flat: the tumbledown fishermen's houses at one fringe, the hard blue jaws of the Pacific at the other. The steely light drained the stones of colour, the colours they would show when the inevitable rain came. Pounded by the surf, the granite ground smooth by millennia of surging tides, they seemed almost monochrome. Nothing bound them together in this one place, yet so distinct were their colours and forms that one of the number would be instantly recognised in the city. 'That's a stone from Birdlings Flat,' would come just as easily from the lips of an observer as could, 'That's a youth from the university.'

The boy, the girl, their homogenous selves. Stones and

youths, all of them, bound by uniformity, a lack of courage and compassion.

They were behind him, still in the car.

If he had any brains, thought Donald, Kieran would get out, have a walk to clear his head. He should be thinking about the things he said, urged on by that dreadful girl.

The old man lifted his stick and waved it, once, to get the boy's attention. In the boot there was a box to fill with stones for the garden. The boy seemed to have forgotten the reason for the trip out.

He must know, thought Donald, that it is impossible for me to gather the stones myself.

Watching the old man against the sky, the girl, huddled under the arm of the boy, said, 'Look at Donald.'

He was trying to bend, one hand grasping the head of his stick, angled like a summer guy-rope. His beard and band of hair gleamed a dull white in the thundery air.

In one swift movement the boy shrank away from her, opened the door and was gone.

'Get the box.' He wouldn't add a 'please'. He wasn't going to beg.

The boy turned and walked back to the car. Donald forced himself up, a stone trophy in his hand, the blood pumping in his forehead, pushing at his temples. Bile had risen in his throat as he'd pushed himself upright. One of his boots had wedged itself in a nest of stones. He dug in the stick and leaned against it, taking his bulk off the trapped leg.

Here was the boy, back with the carton. The girl had remained in the car, though she'd stuck her head out the window and said something sharp to the boy as he'd passed. Just the tone of her voice had reached the old man's ears, the words indistinguishable. It had possibly been only one word, an insult. Women swore a lot these days — words that previously belonged to soldiers. Perhaps women considered themselves to be soldiers; perhaps that was it, he thought, in this muddy, so-called 'war of the sexes'. After the real war, when he'd worked for *The Press*, there was more and more of it, not only in the paper itself — cases of sexual harassment, divorce — but also skirmishes among his colleagues. It irked him; it seemed manufactured, something so utterly removed, in his opinion, from the nuts and bolts of real life. Daphne, for instance — she never saw herself as a soldier.

The boy's face above the carton was set with cold and sadness. The old man's heart pulsed with empathy, for a moment feeling the angst of a young man with a difficult girlfriend.

Get rid of her, he wanted to say. Get rid of that dreadful girl. But numb from waiting for so long in the wind, Donald's lips parted unwillingly and he said nothing.

'You want me to fill the box?' the boy asked, holding up a smooth grey oval. A moa's egg. Donald nodded, looking back towards the car, Japanese, shining, a glow of red between the gunmetal of stone and sky. A plume of cigarette smoke steamed out the window, white, agitated. Normally the spectacle of young women smoking, damaging their beautiful complexions and capacious lungs, distressed him, but in this girl's case and for Kieran's sake, he hoped cancer would come early and rapaciously. Stones clunked into the box.

'We'll make a start on the border today, eh?' he asked the top of Kieran's head. 'For the roses, at the back.'

'If you like,' the boy answered. Exams were over; it was another three days before he caught the plane north.

'Nothing you have to do this afternoon?' Donald asked him.

'Nup,' said the boy.

'What about her?' he asked.

'Who?' The boy squinted up at him in the grey, glary light.

'Your friend.'

'Oh, she'll be all right.'

'I meant . . .' Donald gave up. The boy hadn't understood. Since Daphne left he hadn't liked having women in his house. The only woman he felt comfortable about letting in was the Home Help, who understood that the door to Daphne's room was to remain closed. He cleaned that room himself, dusting around her china-doll collection, the dozen or so of them, the blue multitude of their eyes gazing over his shoulder to the empty single girl's bed. If they had names, he'd never known them. He plumped the scented, heart-shaped, pink lace pillow on her coverlet, gave the tacky knick-knack-cluttered shelves a wipe, around the little men made of shells with their spindly pipe-cleaner arms, the stones with painted-on faces and clothes, the lumpy brown pottery animals. What if Kieran's girlfriend found her way in there? Her curiosity would be horribly aroused. What questions would she ask? It didn't bear thinking about. Donald sighed.

'Are you in pain?' asked the boy. 'I'll do this. You go back to the car.'

'I'm perfectly all right.'

The boy's denim shoulders tensed, then relaxed. His 'suit yourself' hung between them, unspoken, as did the boy's assumption that not only was Donald old, he was difficult. The stones clunked in. The box was nearly full.

'The girl . . .' began Donald.

'Nikki?' Kieran stood and shoved his hands into his pockets.

'Yes. Is she studying history?'

'I think so.'

'You think so? Don't you talk about your studies together?'

'A bit. Yes, she's doing history.' The boy bent to pick up the box.

'Wait a moment,' said Donald. 'There's no hurry.'

'It's freezing, Donald.' Kieran shivered. The older man was warm, with his argyle sweater and tweed jacket. Kieran had dressed for the season it was supposed to be — summer — but the wind was bitter.

'You're all right,' said Donald. 'Is she studying the war?'

'I don't know.' The boy ran his fingers through his hair. He had the kind of androgynous looks women of his generation adored — heavy eyes with dark, curling lashes; full lips; shining auburn hair to his shoulders; long, sensitive hands. Kieran had always been beautiful, even as a child, Donald remembered. He had never been much interested in children but Kieran had always touched his heart, like a favourite nephew, though they were not related.

'She must be, if she knows about the Dresden raids.' Donald had turned, was looking out to sea.

'Don't worry about it, Donald. It doesn't matter.'

The old man shook his head, though the boy's concern for him brought a smile to his lips. Of course it mattered. Nothing at this moment mattered so much. It mattered what the boy had said as well — it wasn't just the girl. Kieran had thought the same. He'd said so: 'If there was another war it would be nuclear and I wouldn't fight.'

'She didn't mean to upset you,' Kieran was saying. 'Let's go back to the car.' He heaved the box on his shoulder and set off, leaning slightly to one side. Donald followed, slowly, so that he wouldn't have to wait with the girl while the box was stowed in the boot.

'Here,' he said, at the car. 'You drive.' He threw the boy the keys. Catching them, Kieran grinned. He enjoyed driving and Donald never hassled him about breaking the speed limit: War Heroes liked speed, and Donald was a War Hero; he'd flown the Lancaster Bombers.

Donald didn't want the girl and Kieran side by side in the back seat as they had been on the way out to the Flats, whispering, the girl giggling at his claudicant driving, his damaged foot always too heavy on the accelerator and brake. It wasn't until he had clumped around to the other side of the Mazda that he noticed the girl had climbed through to the front and was sitting in the passenger seat. She'd been there for some time, judging by the sweet wrappers scattered on her lap — his sweet wrappers, from his supply of barley sugars in the glovebox. Kieran had his arm hooked around her neck and was kissing her, full on the lips. Her orange spiky hair stood straight up, so short Donald could see her scalp in places. He opened the back door and got in. There was less legroom in the back — he'd be lucky if he didn't get cramp on the way back to Christchurch.

The girl rested her hand on Kieran's thigh and the boy drove like a maniac. Donald forced himself to look out the side window and found himself thinking about Daphne. At the beginning she'd displayed her affection for him like that — laid her palm on his thigh whenever they went out driving. He'd scarcely felt it through the scar tissue, the thick, burnt skin; there was just the vague sensation of warmth, an awareness of the weight of her hand lying there, peaceful, trusting. She'd wait patiently while he made his way to her side of the car to open her door; she accepted his courting gifts and billets-doux with the grace and delight of a fifties debutante. She'd loved his manners, his olde worlde courtesy. His stories of the war fascinated her; he hadn't felt the need to censor the more horrific details as a soldier had to with some women of her mother's — his own — generation. Twenty-eight years between them, but it hadn't seemed like much, even with her room being the way it was. Perhaps a psychologist would view her obsessions with dolls and little men made of shells and painted stones as arrested. Donald himself, when pain impelled him to cease his doll dusting and rest a while on her bed, found them a little macabre, especially now she'd gone and left it all with him. Perhaps he should give them all to Nikki, though she didn't seem the doll type.

They'd reached the turn-off, where the road went one way towards Akaroa, the other back to Christchurch. Hardly pausing, Kieran swung the car out into the empty road. Donald supposed he'd judged the intersection first. The boy's reflexes were wired, quick-fire, more so with that hand on his thigh. Daphne could tell a lot about people from their hands. What would she have made of Nikki's? The one on Kieran's leg was broad, coarse-skinned, with large, round knuckles. There was something determined — bloody-minded even — about it.

'You okay back there, Donald?' Kieran asked. Donald could see his mouth moving in the rear-vision mirror, the boy's white, even teeth, saliva clear as spring water.

'I'm perfectly all right,' said Donald, for the second time that day. Nikki had twisted in her seat and was looking at him, her eyes narrowed. He supposed she meant to look concerned, but the overall effect was one of antagonism. It was synchronised, like formation flying, the way they both glanced away from each other at exactly the same moment.

Having slowed enough to take the corner, Kieran opened the car up and ran it smoothly through its gears until the speedo

— not that Donald could quite see it — must have read a hundred and ten at least. It was like being in a plane — a modern plane, not one of the Bombers.

Sometimes he still woke in a sweat, the Rear Gunner's scream bounding off his quiet suburban walls as he was burnt alive, trapped in his metal cage as they landed, the back of the plane on fire. They couldn't get him out, that poor bastard in the metal cage, so they shot him. It was because — he'd told Daphne on the first night she'd heard him screaming, when he heard the Rear Gunner still screaming thirty-six years after they'd put him out of his misery — it was because of the way they'd built the planes. The Gunner sat in a kind of mesh enclosure, made of a single, perforated piece of metal bent into a dome. It wasn't a true mesh, so there were no weak links that might break apart with the heat.

As they'd dragged Donald from the plane, afire from foot to waist, he'd heard the shot, a single shot through the flames to the frantic, wavering, blackened figure inside. For the men gathered on the dark airstrip, an English dawn breaking behind the flaring plane, that single shot stopped the screaming. For Donald, half-crazed with pain as they rolled him on the tarmac to douse the flames, the screaming went on, night after night, on and on.

'There, there,' Daphne had said on so many occasions, slipping into bed beside him, holding him, making no demands. She knew, from his burns, that her demands could never be met, even if she'd had them. Sometime during the night she'd depart, light-footed as a night nurse, back down the hall to her innocent room.

'Kieran!'

Donald opened his eyes to see Nikki gesturing towards him in the back seat.

'Am I going too fast?' Kieran asked, laughing. 'You had your eyes closed.'

'I'm a little tired.' He sounded tetchy, he knew. 'Not really in the mood for company.'

'We'll go then, as soon as we get to your place.' Kieran took Nikki's hand from his thigh and dropped it in her lap. 'Sorry, Donald.'

It was all wrong. The boy was not only apologising for accompanying him to Birdlings Flat when the trip together had been Donald's idea in the first place, but feeling embarrassed about his girlfriend's hand. Perhaps it had been a little higher than when first she'd laid it there, but Donald knew the urge to touch all the time, he knew Nikki's hunger, he knew what it was to be unable to satisfy it.

'Home!' Kieran zapped the car up the drive and into the garage, a swift, precise manoeuvre that at its abrupt conclusion had all three of them straining at the full extent of their seatbelts, like dogs on leads. Nikki giggled.

'You're terrible, Kieran,' she said.

Donald's thigh muscle went into a violent cramp. He let out an involuntary moan. Kieran started.

'What is it?'

'Leg. Cramp.'

He should have told the boy to park the car in the driveway, then he would only have had to do battle with the branches of the overgrown rhododendron. As it was, in the garage, it was a struggle for Kieran to get him out of the back seat, stand him up and help him to walk the cramp off. By the time they made it outside the girl was there, at the rear of the car, trying to take his other arm. He shook her off. The cramp made him impatient, or honest, or both. Kieran unlocked the front door and they made their way into his quiet hall, the cramp loosening its jaws, and into the living room.

'Do you want to sit down?' Kieran asked, solemn, concerned. Nikki stood dead centre, staring around. Through his pain, Donald watched her and wondered what she was thinking. Daphne had said he had no idea of colour and design. Everything was beige — the carpet, the walls, the ceiling, the furniture. To Donald they toned in: the colour was what made the room peaceful.

'I'd rather stand for a moment.' He couldn't care less what Nikki thought.

'I'll put the jug on, shall I?' Kieran disappeared into the kitchen.

Nikki was looking at him with those narrowed eyes again. It occurred to him that perhaps she was focusing, that it was not concern nor antagonism, but short-sightedness.

'Is there something you can take?' she asked.

'I beg your pardon?' He shifted on his stick.

'A pill or something. To help.'

'There are only two remedies for muscular cramp. Walk it off or wait it out.'

'Quinine,' said the girl. 'Soldiers suffering from malaria in the war, they were given quinine to help with the cramp.'

'Ah. The war again. You know a lot about it, do you?'

'A bit.' The girl looked uncomfortable. She shot a glance towards the kitchen. From the clatter of china it seemed Kieran was doing the breakfast dishes. Donald wished he wouldn't. The Home Help was due at three; she'd run out of things to do.

'You're studying the war?' The cramp had almost gone now, he could sit down, but cramps were like earthquakes — they gave out aftershocks. He didn't want the girl to have to help him up again.

'Not exactly, no,' she answered slowly. 'I'm doing a paper called Women and War. How we were affected, you know.'

'"We"? You were never in a war.'

'No, but . . .' The girl trailed off, gazing at the kitchen door like a stunned mullet.

'But what?' Donald persisted. The girl turned her eyes on him. They glittered with health, blue and white.

'But I can still empathise with what woman went through. Rape and so on.'

Donald raised his eyebrows. 'It's women, with an "e",' he said tartly, 'and rape was the least of it.' He could sit down now. He made his way to the chair. The girl was there before him, extending a tentative hand. He ignored it, and sat heavily.

'That's not what our lecturer said.' The girl spoke in a rush. 'She said that women aren't remembered for the sacrifices we made, that our names aren't on the cenotaph. We're the forgotten casualties of —'

'"She"?' interrupted Donald. '"She's" a lecturer in history?'

'In the Women's Studies Department.' The girl offered no explanation as to what that department was, nor to what faculty it belonged. Kieran came through with three mugs of tea.

'What on earth is the Women's Studies Department?' asked Donald. He had a sudden vague memory of some women disrupting the Anzac celebrations two or three years ago, tipping blood on the stone, upsetting the old diggers. He wondered if Nikki remembered. Perhaps he should ask her — perhaps she could fill him in on the details. She was gazing with a kind of drugged intensity into the steam of her tea.

'I'll down this,' said Kieran, raising his cup, 'then I'll make a start on the border. The roses around the back, you said?'

Donald nodded, sipping. Taking her cup with her, Nikki had

crossed to the chiffonier, an oblong of pale beige oak, and was examining its single adornment, a photograph. It was of Daphne, taken in the summer of 1976. She wore a broad, flower-brimmed hat, a warm sea sparkling behind her.

'Who's that?' asked Nikki. 'She looks lovely.'

'An old friend of Donald's,' said Kieran.

'Ooo — an old girlfriend, Donald?' asked Nikki, playfully. 'Was she your lover?'

Though he could scarcely believe it himself, Donald was blushing. That dreadful girl, boots and all, never pausing to think. What if Daphne had died? The girl would never have thought of that, would she? That Daphne may have died and any mention of her was torture to him?

'I should prune that rhodo back for you. It's out over the driveway.' Kieran gave the girl an irritated look, but she didn't notice. She still had her back to them, examining the photograph.

'That'd be good.' Donald wished the girl would come away. 'Do that first.'

'That's at Birdlings Flat!' she exclaimed. 'You can tell by the stones.'

'Daphne loved Birdlings Flat. She used to collect stones there and paint them. You remember that fad, Kieran, for pet rocks? When you were a little boy. Daphne made her own.' Shut up, Donald, he told himself. It was relief from the cramp finally releasing — it made him loquacious.

'Vaguely,' said Kieran. 'I vaguely remember it. You finished?' He held out his hand for Nikki's cup. Obligingly she handed it to him, though it was still half full.

'Was it a long relationship, yours and Daphne's?' the girl was asking. 'Did she live here with you?'

Donald glared at Kieran — shut the girl up.

'Shut up,' Kieran hissed at her, gratifyingly, on his way through to the kitchen with the cups. The girl made a strange noise like a hiccup and glanced wildly around. It was her turn to blush. Once again her eyes settled on the photograph.

'She looks like a Daphne,' she said coyly. 'If you hadn't told me her name, I could have guessed it.'

How fatuous, thought Donald. He angled his body in the chair to look out the window. There was a flash of blue as Kieran passed between the garage and the garden shed, emerging a few seconds later with the pruning shears.

'Just the lower branches!' called Donald, fumbling with the window. 'Kieran! Just the lower branches!'

Kieran nodded. 'Yup.'

Donald watched him for a moment, then relaxed into his chair with his tea. The dregs, still lukewarm. He took a mouthful, then put down the cup . . . the girl! How peculiar — he'd thought she was still beside the photograph, he'd sensed her to still be there, not that he'd cast his attention in that direction. He hadn't wanted to encourage her. But she wasn't there, just Daphne in her hat, with the sea. Donald's heart pounded. The girl must be in Daphne's room! She wasn't with Kieran, he could see that, so she must be in Daphne's room.

From the down the hall he heard the lavatory flush. He listened for her footsteps, down the hall, into the living room.

'Top-up, Donald?' She was right beside his chair, reaching for his cup.

'No, thanks,' said Donald. He needed to go to the loo himself, in private. Perhaps he could put the girl to work.

'Why don't you get the box of stones out of the boot?' he asked. 'You're a big strong girl.'

'Sure. Is it unlocked?'

'Yes, off you go,' he dismissed her. She went.

After one failed attempt, Donald lurched to his feet, retrieved his stick from where it leaned against the back of his chair and made his slow progress to the bathroom. It was on his way back, his legs aching, feet burning, the tendons in his groin threatening to snap like perished rubber bands, sheer force of will being the only thing sliding each foot after the other, that he heard raised voices.

'I didn't!' the girl was shrieking. 'I didn't!'

'You did! You're so fucking nosy!' from the boy.

In the living room Donald leaned against the back of his chair, concealed behind the curtain, watching them. The girl held the heavy box in her arms.

'I just asked if she was his girlfriend.' She'd lowered her voice slightly.

'It was none of your business. You never know when to stop. Why don't you piss off?' Kieran was waving the pruning shears.

'No!' There was a clatter as the shears hit the ground and their bodies connected. The box was knocked to one side, the stones rolling like heavy apples onto the concrete. It was the girl who initiated it, pushing Kieran. Donald felt a surge of indignation for the boy, which was quickly followed by disgust: Kieran pulled back, rolled a hand into a fist, and struck the girl hard on the side of the head. She fell to the ground, curled up like a hedgehog.

If they'd been children Donald would have rapped on the window and waved an admonishing finger at them. But they weren't children. He was rooted to the spot, frozen, as if the chill winds of the Flat had followed him home to Cashmere. He thought of all the times he'd wanted to hit Daphne, when she was irritating, when she'd needled him, during their last years together. He never had. Perhaps he should have.

The girl was moving. She crawled on her hands and knees to the front step.

'Oh, for Christ's sake!' said Kieran. 'Have some fucking pride.'

Nikki buried her face in her hands and sobbed. It was a quiet sobbing — Donald couldn't hear her, but her shoulders heaved and sighed. Kieran came to her and grabbed her roughly by one arm. Turning her head away, as if she feared another blow, the girl screamed in high soprano, 'Leave me alone!'

Donald saw that she hadn't been crying at all, not really. Her face was dry. The boy saw it, too. Her threw her arm away like a stick and bent towards her, his face ugly, strained.

'That's exactly what I want to do. I didn't want you to come to the Flat in the first place. Fuck off!'

If he didn't sit down right now, Donald thought, he would fall over. He took a step around the side of his chair, warning himself not to look out the window. He didn't want them to know he'd been watching — what would they think? An old man watching them fight. It was almost as voyeuristic as if he'd watched them make love.

From two or three yards away, through the glass, Kieran was looking at him. The older man met his eyes; he couldn't stop himself. The girl stayed huddled between them while the men stared at each other. Kieran smiled. It was a sort of half smile — complicitous, a smile that meant 'Women!' and 'What we men have to put up with!'

Donald turned his back on him and sank into his chair. What was all that? It hadn't seemed real — the dry tears, the beautiful face of the boy screwed up, tense as a fist.

With the sound of running feet he dared to look out again.

The girl was wheeling her bicycle out of his garage, really crying now, with her nose running. There was a graze on her temple, a bead of blood on a spike of orange hair. Outside his window she threw herself astride the saddle. Full of tears, her eyes searched the window before she found him.

'Goodbye,' she mouthed, then she rode away, disappeared.

Kieran was standing beside him, his guilty hands shoved into his pockets. Donald wouldn't look at him. He sat with his stick between his legs, turning it round and round, screwing its rubber end into the carpet.

'You won't fight in a war, but you'll hit a woman,' he said eventually. Kieran's eyes bored into the top of his bald head. The boy probably thought he was a specious old fool. He said nothing to defend himself, at any rate.

'You're a coward,' said Donald, 'aren't you?'

'I suppose so.' Kieran spoke evenly. 'I'm sorry, Donald.'

'It's not me you should be apologising to!' Donald exploded. 'Go home. I've had enough for one day.'

Kieran's footsteps led towards the hall and stopped. 'I wasn't apologising for myself. I meant, I'm sorry she asked all those stupid questions.'

'She's young, curious. It's natural. I didn't mind,' Donald lied. He swivelled in his seat, but the boy had gone. He'd left while Donald was still speaking. A moment later, silver flashed at the corner of his eye as the boy's bicycle rolled away, after the girl, down the drive.

It wasn't until much later, at three, when he got up to let in the Home Help, that he noticed the door to Daphne's room was open.

'Coming!' he called to the Home Help, making his way to

close it. So the girl had gone in. She'd had a look around. Nothing had been moved, he didn't think. The Home Help knocked again and Donald noticed that there was something different about one of the dolls. Its head had been turned towards the door. It was a doll with yellow hair and rosebud mouth, staring him full in the face as he stood in the threshold. He turned away, leaving the door open.

'There's a carton lying out on the drive,' he told the Help. 'Pack up those dolls, and the little men made of shells, would you?'

'Dolls?' She looked puzzled. She took off her coat.

'In the other bedroom. There are a whole lot of dolls. Give them to the City Mission, or whoever.'

In the garden Donald waited on the bench under the willow so that he wouldn't be able to hear the clunk of china heads going into the box, the rustle of their dresses. When Daphne had left, run away with her young man, it was to lead a proper woman's life. In her life with Donald, her battles with him, the dolls had been her foot soldiers, proof of her girlhood, her virginity. It was, he supposed, a kind of deprivation she'd practised on him: where his war wounds would have allowed him some kind of adult affection, the dolls prevented it. Could he have told Nikki all this? If he'd done so, kept her talking in the room with him, then he never would have lost Kieran. Perhaps Nikki, from her youthful, idealistic standpoint, would have shed some light on Daphne, helped him to understand . . . but that was a fantasy, and Donald had never been one for that.

At five o'clock the Help called from the front steps, 'Goodbye, Mr Outhwaite! Dinner's in the oven — see you tomorrow!' Donald made his weary way inside. In Daphne's room she had done exactly as she was asked. The dolls were gone, and the little men made of shells. Only the stones remained, ranged along the windowsill, their painted features fading. Like him they were returning, slowly, quietly, to their lost, ambiguous selves.

The Night I Got My Tuckie

Whenever Dad wants a drink, which is most nights, we have to drive across the town line — just him and me in the pickup like we hardly never used to when Mom was alive. Sometimes he tells me to change my sweater or wipe my face, but most nights he hardly even looks at me before we climb on up and drive on out of Zion. Some nights it's south we go, to Al's Bar, which has its northern wall along the boundary. One time I worked that out for myself, following along directly from the sign on the road — ZION TOWN LINE — the heel of one pink Barbie shoe hard against the toe of the other in a dead-straight line from the sign on the sidewalk until I come up against the Al's brown concrete corner. That was years ago I did that. Don't even fit those Barbie shoes no more.

Other nights we go north, which is further to drive, across the Illinois-Wisconsin border. There's a place there by the harbor Dad's partial to, and I don't mind it either. I mind it better than

Al's, which is low-slung in its ceiling and thick with nasty air, a stink of smoke and spilled beer. Shame, but we go to Al's more often, it being easier on Dad's wallet and less miles to cover home.

The bar in Wisconsin's called Harbor Lights, which is funny, because there's no lights you can see from there — you wouldn't even know how close the harbor is 'less you took a big lungful in the carpark, and then you might get a whiff of lake weed. In the summer you can see boats towed by on the road and that'd tell you, but only if you were watching through the window.

Harbor Lights is white and made of wood on the outside like a nice house. It's got shutters that don't shut and a pot of plastic flowers on a hook by the main door. Dad allus parks his pickup by the hook, so's if I gets tired, I can curl up on the seat and look at the flowers. Once or twice I've seen night-bugs snooping in the petals, like they were being tricked by them and thought they were real. First time I saw them I showed Candy who works in the bar — I got right out of the truck and went right back in and asked her to come and look and Candy said a funny thing. She said, 'Ruthie, those bugs are as foolish as men are — least my husband's got a lot in common with those bugs. He don't know what's real either.' Her husband had just left her then — this was years and years ago, at least two, when I was nine — and all Candy would say about that was two things:

1) Jed had the brains of a bug and
2) his new girl was fake, like the flowers: fake tits, fake hair, fake teeth.

Candy only has fake fingernails and phony eyelashes, which are silvery blue and so heavy her eyes are always half closed.

The point of all this is to show you the setting, kind of, so you can see where it happened, the night I got my tuckie. It was a Tuesday and Dad and me, the minute we parked, saw the car. It was a new shiny green Ford, one we'd never seen there before. Winter was coming on, so it wasn't the time for tourists, people coming up from Chicago to swim in the lake or go fishing for trout. There's good fishing in Zion, particularly round the power station where the water used for cooling the turbines comes out warm. They'd all cluster round there and pull out giant fish — Dad says he wouldn't eat 'em if you paid him a million. Anyways, it was too darn cold for that now, and I knew it was cold — that's why I had Pink Panther with me. He's taller'n I am and he's good for a blanket or a pillow in the pickup if Dad stays thirsty for longer. Dad thinks I'm getting too old for Pinkie, but he lets me cart him still. This particular night I took him in the bar. He's useful in there — I'm stunted for my age, 'cording to Candy, and if I put him on the bar-stool, then sit on top of him, it's comfy and high. It was Candy's idea for me to do that, years and years ago.

We went in, Dad, the Panther and me, and there was Candy behind the bar, peering through the silvery-blue strings of her eyelashes, red fingernails clinking on the beer-taps. The lights were on, glowing on the wood paneling around the windows. The wall behind where Candy stands is glass shelves of different kinds of drinks, all colors — red, blue, green, brown, black and clear — with a mirror behind them. One time Candy'd tucked her skirt into her panties and it was all hooked up at the back and 'cause I could see her fanny reflected in the mirror, flickering through clear spirits, the gin and vodka and Bacardi, I could tell her. She was so grateful 'cause I just leaned across and whispered — I didn't say it right out loud so's all the men could hear. She gave me a Coke, which I'd earned. Most often she and me're the only females 'cause the women round here drink alone at home, while the men drink together. Know which I'd prefer — makes me wish I'd been born a man, though there's plenty of reasons to be wishin' for that, that's for sure.

This night Candy and me had company. There was another woman. She was sitting in one of the booths at the side, the ones Candy had done out in red leatherette after Jed left her. I could tell the woman wasn't from around here. For a start off, she had a braid, brown and gray and mousy, down her back. And she had a man with her — her husband, it turned out — and he matched her exactly. Not that he had a braid, but his hair was the exact same color, though bushy and curly. They had the exact same blue eyes, sticky-out like the strangest of the trout they pull up round the plant. They were just sitting there, him and her, face to face, staring at their beers, and she was pointed our way, so I got a good look at her. If she'd had necklaces and earrings I might've thought she was a hippy from California or Canada or such — we get them sometimes — but she had nothing like that, just a rollneck sweater in a bad shade of brown, like an old hamburger pattie, and no make-up — not a scratch. Nails weren't done either; they were as plain as little shells on her stumpy fingers, turning her beer glass round and round. Women round here wouldn't never go out with plain nails — it'd be like strollin' down the main street 'out your pants on.

I sat up there at the bar with Candy on the other side and stared at the lady, while Dad went and sat with his friends Chuck and Bob. At Al's sometimes he plays the one-armed bandits but Harbor Lights is more high class and they have nothing like that, they just got Chuck and Bob like permanent fixtures. Bob's all right; Chuck I don't like. When he comes to the bar he squeezes my thigh hard down to the bone and puts his dirty hand on my hair. Candy tells him off — she says, she's just a child, you leave it out. If Candy's busy serving drinks I try to narrow my eyes and stare him down just the way she does, though on account of having no false lashes I'm not as good at it as she is and mostly Chuck laughs and says how I'm getting prettier every day and how he'll be my first. First what, I allus think, and stare at myself through the bottles and think he's a liar. I ain't pretty — I'm too skinny and my hair sticks up no matter how I comb it.

This night, the night I'm telling you about, Candy wasn't too busy to tell Chuck off and she told him off good. I slipped off Pinkie, tied his arms round my neck and went over to the booth next to the lady with the braid. It didn't take her long to notice me watchin' her over the top of the red leatherette.

'Hello,' she said, 'what's your name?' She had a sweet, soft voice — nearly a stupid voice, which came from right at the back of her throat, but I could tell from her eyes she wasn't dumb. They were those bright, glinty kind of eyes clever people have, and now that I was up close they were more gray than blue. Her husband swivelled round. 'Oh,' he said, 'we have company.' And no surprise he had the same voice, only deeper. They were so alike they could've been toys hatched out of the same plastic egg. They were McDonald's toys from the same day, same week.

'Where're you from?' I asked them. Wherever it was, they saw a lot of sun. The man had creases round his eyes deep enough to hide your finger in, but he was maybe only the same age as Dad. 'Nyu Zillun,' the man said. He put his hand in his pocket and pulled out a little green monster with hopeless crippled legs and saucer eyes. It was made of plastic, but it wasn't a Pokemon. 'A tuckie,' said the lady, as he gave it to me.

'You keep it,' said the man.

'What's it for?' I turned it over. A tuckie from Nyu Zillun. 'What's it used for?' It had a hole in the top of its head. The lady looked at the man.

'Well,' she said, 'you can put a string through here and wear it around your neck.'

'We've got big ones like this at home, at Mardi people's meeting houses,' said Ray.

'Real ones?' I asked.

The lady nodded and said sternly to her husband, 'Those aren't tuckies, Ray, those are tekoteko.'

I made a promise to myself never to go to Nyu Zillun, wherever it is. Maybe these Mardis keep these tuckies as pets and they're probably real bad-tempered. With little bent legs like this they can't possibly run around; they'd be bored and grouchy like my mother was. Maybe they shoot at them for sport and that's why they've got holes in their heads.

'Is that your dad?' The lady pointed at Chuck.

'Christ, no,' I said, and out of habit looked round to see if anybody had heard me. In Harbor Lights you can cuss all you like. In Zion you can't — they're real religious. You can't buy a drink and you don't say Christ 'less you're praying. My dad used to be religious, but after Mom died he was that mad at God he gave it away.

'Where's your mum?' asked the lady. I shrugged. Who knows the answer to that one? Her last year she was as mean as a cross-eyed snake. Maybe she's gone to hell.

'You should ask her to wash your hair,' the lady said, though she was looking at my fingers, which were smeary, now I looked at them.

'For heaven's sake, Kathy,' muttered Ray, then, 'You can't help yourself, can you?'

'Is that your mother?' Now she was pointing at Candy, and I don't know what made me do it, but I nodded. 'Course I used to wish Candy was my mother, maybe because I saw more of her than any other lady, least since Dad took me out of Zion

School — 'cause of all the claptrap, he said.

'Kathy,' the man sounded tetchy, 'it's none of your business. Have a break from it, will you?'

'Why have you come to Zion?' I asked, forgetting for a moment that we'd crossed the town line and weren't in Zion at all.

'We're on our way to Wisconsin,' said Kathy, 'to visit my sister. She's married to a farmer there. We've driven up from Chicago.'

'Oh, I'd sure like to go to Chicago,' I told them. Even though it's so close to Zion we never went there, Dad and I, because Dad isn't much of a traveler. Over the top of her beer glass Kathy widened her eyes like Candy can't never do. Maybe she thought it was weird I'd never been. 'I got no cause to go there, though,' I added, because that's what Dad says. Kathy pushed her glass towards her husband like she wanted another beer. He read the signs and went to the bar while the tuckie danced around on Pinkie's nose.

'Welcome to the family,' said Pinkie. He doesn't talk much and I was so taken up with listening to him I hardly noticed Kathy was talking again.

'In Nyu Zillun I look after kuds like you,' she was saying.

'What's a kud?'

'Girls like you,' she went on, 'who might be having a hard time at home.' She kept flicking her eyes over to the bar to make sure her husband wasn't coming back yet, like she didn't want him to hear.

'The Welfare, you mean?' I asked her. I checked on Dad. He was doing the usual thing, lining up his empties on the table, him and Bob and Chuck just sitting and staring at a spot above each other's heads, like a fly was hovering there or something. He wouldn't like me talking to Welfare.

'You must spend a lot of time in here, eh?' she said, 'with your mother working as a barmaid.'

I nodded. It was interesting being Candy's daughter.

'When we get home at night she makes me a Chocomilk,' I told her, and it was lovely, snuggled up with Candy on the sofa, sleepy and warm, Pinkie and the tuckie and Candy and me.

'Have you got a father?' Kathy asked, quickly. Her husband was nearly finished at the bar; he was paying Candy for the beers.

'Christ, no. He ran off with a girl with false titties,' I told her, 'and not only that, but she'd had injections in her lips so she'd be better at kissing him and what all. That's what Mom told me.'

Kathy's eyes spronged out of her head.

'But she doesn't miss him at all, on account of him having the brains of a night-bug.'

Kathy laughed then, and all the skin round her eyes and mouth loosened up, like it was worry that had held it tight before. I smiled back at her and put the tuckie away in my jeans pocket. 'Would you like me to write you a letter from Nyu Zillun?' she asked.

'What for?'

'Here.' She took a pen and notebook out of her bag. 'You write down your address and I'll send you a pretty card. How old are you, dear?'

'Eleven.' I used the back of Pinkie's head to press on. He didn't mind so much, especially now I'd put the tuckie away in my pocket. I guess he thought it was being disrespectful, jumping up and down on his nose like that.

'That's an interesting way to spell Ezekiel,' Kathy said, 'and Avenue.'

'Spelling schmelling,' I said. That's Dad's joke — he can't spell neither. But the lady raised her eyebrows like a schoolteacher. The froth on the two beer glasses wobbled as Ray set them down.

'Would you like a Coke or a limonade, young Whoosit?' he asked.

'No thanks,' I said, straight away. Never accept anything from anybody, Dad says. There's hardly anyone left who thinks this way now, everybody's a charity case, he says, the world makes it that way, but we ain't and never shall be Amen.

But my mouth watered.

'Have you had your tea yet?' asked Kathy.

'Tea?' I asked.

'Your evening meal,' she said, and her husband talked over the top of her, saying, 'Here endeth the interrogation. We're on holiday, for chrissake.'

'Oh — do you look after kuds like me who might be heving a hard toime too?' I asked him, all wide-eyed and innocent like I didn't realize I was mimicking his old wife. I'm the best at that — I used to mimic our pastor and have Dad in stitches. Maybe I helped Dad lose his respect for him.

There was thunder in the air. I used to smell it when Mom and Dad were going to fight. Best thing is to tie Pinkie's paws back round your neck and heave off someplace else.

'See ya,' I said.

I went to the pickup and lay down on Pinkie for a pillow and turned the tuckie over and over in the light. At the edges the green plastic was thin and glowing and tasty-looking. I put it in my mouth and sucked it like a candy.

After a while Chuck came out and tried all the doors but I'd locked them, of course. I only needed to wake up with him slobbering all over me once to learn that lesson.

'You go out there at night, you lock all the doors,' Candy told me afterwards.

Chuck mouthed bad words at me through the glass but I

just ignored him. Pinkie put his head up, though, and danced rudely around, back and forth. He allus does that until Chuck shuts up and goes away. Then Pinkie did a terrible fart on account of having had a whole mini-sak of Dunkin' Donuts for supper and I had to wind the window down a crack. I'm mighty glad I did, because otherwise I wouldn't have heard the Nyu Zillunites.

'So she was lying?' Kathy was saying, her voice all trembly.

'Like a pro,' said Ray. 'Her father told me all about it in the men's room. Mother died two years ago of cancer. Lot of it round here and the locals think it's because of the power plant. Leaks, apparently.' There was a pause then. I could hear their car keys jangling.

'And?' said Kathy.

'So the kud lives with her father. He drinks a lot — but I think he loves her.' The car doors opened. 'Doesn't send her to school, though.'

'I'll ring them from Wisconsin,' said Kathy.

'Ring who? It's none of your business!'

'Ring whoever it is who takes care of cases like this —' and maybe she kept talking then, but I couldn't hear her, because the doors shut. They drove away.

I never got a pretty card from her and so far Welfare haven't been on our case any more than normal. Might be because I never told her my name. I've still got the tuckie — I did what she said and tied it round my neck. Now and then I worry about those real tuckies and wonder if Kathy looks after them too. They can't have much of a life, lying round with their useless legs and being shot at by the Mardis. This little guy has a much better time, right here in Zion, with me.

Oy Joy

Some nights I can hear him calling from out in the bay, from beyond the Big Rock. If I said that to anyone, like old Valmai down the beach; if I told her that after a few gins, or at least after she'd had enough gins to shut up and listen to me, she'd say, 'It's just the wind.'

Some nights when I hear him it is windy, but some nights it's as still as the swamp, black, the sky showing starry in the sea. Besides, the call isn't 'Woo–ooo' like in Pommy fairy stories or Yank cartoons; it's not like a mermaid or a ghost or something; it's more like a bark — a harsh, deep, double-shot 'Au Au!' I hear it like that, the first time anyway. The second time it might be clearer: 'Oy Oy'. If it goes on after that he goes the extra mile and puts in the J: 'Oy Joy!'

He used to call me a lot when he was alive — call me from down the beach if he wanted a knife or something, if he was gutting the fish, or if he wanted the sharpening stone. Or if he'd forgotten the scaler, or needed a clean bucket to bring the fish up to the house. He'd call me from down on the beach, below the pohutukawas, under the cliffs, 'Oy Joy!' He was a big man with a loud voice — not particularly deep, but the sort of voice that could carry through reinforced concrete or a strong offshore westerly, if he wanted it to. Penetrating is what you'd call it.

'Joy!' And I'd slap on my hat double-quick so's not to annoy him, tie it on under my chin for the wind and hurry down to see what he wanted. He'd have all the catch in the bottom of the boat, pulled up on the hard sand, thirty-pound schnappers sometimes. He was a good fisherman, though I wouldn't say he had a feel for it. When you have a feel for something you have a bit of compassion — you know, the fishermen who have a feel for it always knock a struggling fish on the head to put it out of its misery. The only time I ever saw Barry put something out of its misery it was an octopus he'd got in the net. By the time I got down to the beach he had it laid out on the hard sand and was bashing it with the gaffer. It didn't wriggle around; it just lay there while he bashed its poor, heavy, shining, purple head, bloody on the sand.

'Why're you killing that, Barry?' I asked him. We weren't going to eat it — no need to, with all that schnapper. Besides, Barry thought octopus was wog food.

He'd looked up at me then — I'd broken his murderous concentration — and it was so pathetic, really, what the octopus did. It reached up with one of its clammy legs, reached up and softly curled around the hand that held the gaffer, like it was pleading for mercy. It was as if the octopus and I were thinking the same thing as we looked at Barry. He gave up then: stood and kicked the thing back into the waves. Don't suppose it lived — they've got soft heads, octopuses, and he'd been at it a while before I came down.

Oy Joy. I've been hearing it a lot more lately, since my son bought me the remote for the TV, the thing you point at it to shut up the ads. Some nights I don't bother with it. The TV's around the corner from the kitchen, so I wouldn't be able to hear the ads finish and I might miss a bit of my programme. That's why I never put the mute on if I'm getting my tea. Tea usually takes two ad breaks if I put the kettle on in the first one. In the second one I have to move quickly, slap a bit of corned beef or luncheon sausage on a plate and a tomato or something. Never fish. I don't eat fish any more and it's a blessed relief. I was sick of the taste — all those ruddy schnapper and parore and kingis and flounder from over at the river. It wasn't just the taste, though. There were other reasons for why I'd started to gag at the sight of it — the boat coming in laden, summer and winter, oh yes. I'd given it up before he died. Quite a while. Since the octopus. That's why Barry had killed it, you see, because it had been eating his fish in the net. I decided it could have my fish, all the fish it wanted.

It's when I'm sitting quiet, though, and using my new thing to shut off the ads, that's when I hear it. Doesn't matter which way the wind is, which side of the house the windows are open: 'Oy!' — impatient.

Barry, Barry! Sometimes I answer him, not out loud, just in my head, while the cleaning fluids and cars and kids in nappies flash on the telly. It's better to answer him, I've found, then he shuts up for a bit. Otherwise he goes on and on, when I'm tucked up in bed at the other end of the big fibro house — 'Oy Joy!' I suppose I could ask him what he wants.

I've always been an anxious person, not the sort of person people are drawn to. The look of me gives it away — I *look* anxious: thin, pale, hunched over worse now the old bones have started to crumble. Always sickening for something. Drove Barry wild. I've been better since he died. Still not an ounce of flesh on me, though.

'Christ, Joy,' he said once, some time in the seventies, 'you've got less flesh on you than a leatherjacket.'

Slept in the spare room after that, like I still do. Nothing would induce me to move back, even though he's dead, though most would say the main room view's a better one. It's got the sea and Big Rock. From my room there's a view of the brown hills, a line of pines and the front end of the farmer's place, his boat and dogs, flash car. It's the dry view I prefer. Besides, it stinks of fish in the main bedroom, like a bit of bait's rolled out of his pocket, or a fish eye's come unblobbed from his shirt and dropped under the duchess. Like it always used to smell, even though I scrubbed the room out after he died.

My son comes up here every few days from his place down on the beach, to mow the lawn on his little ride-on mower, and after he's driven round and round on the lawn he comes inside and cleans his dad's room. There's nothing Rex likes more than cleaning a room that's already clean, or mowing a lawn that's already shaved nearly bare. He's a good, clean boy, not afraid of soap and water, though he's seeing too much of old Valmai and her gin bottle. I've seen him from up here, going into her place at eleven in the morning, staggering out after three to go home and sleep it off. Then he wakes up and makes his tea and watches telly, cleaning bits of his house during the ad breaks.

He's come up today, Rex has, though I haven't told him what happened on the beach this morning. He doesn't even know I went down the beach when it was just light.

'Oy Joy!' It had been going on all night, so often that I stuffed the new thing down the cushions and let the ads blare. Barry got quite frantic — never sounded any closer, though. You'd think, if it was his spirit or whatever, it'd come in, it'd cross the bay and zoom in like his tin dinghy used to, laden, low in the water. Tried to tell myself to be with Valmai on this one, what she said, that it's probably the wind, whistling through a hole in Big Rock; that it's a trick of the wind, the wind being a clever dick — it's not something it does normally, not loud enough to hear it from the other side of the bay. And if it was Barry, wouldn't he come up to the house, stand invisible behind my chair, before leaning forward to whisper 'Oy Joy'? I might even get a warning he was there before he said anything — get a whiff of him, salt or grog. If it was him he'd come up here, wouldn't he? If it was me he was calling.

Anyway, last night it kept up after I'd gone to bed, read a bit of my library book and turned out the light. Even though I told myself it was only the wind, it unsettled me. I was unsettled, tossed and turned, got up, went to the lav, went back to bed, turned on the light, read a bit more, listened out.

Oy Joy.

It was a thunderclap that woke me, between here and the hills, above the land, empty dry thunder. I went across the hall to the main bedroom to see if the weather was coming in from the sea. It wasn't raining yet, but the sky had that heavy purple look like it might. It was more a night sky, more as if the sun was about to go down behind the hills in the west, rather than rise above Big Rock in the east; more like it was the end of the day than the beginning of one.

Barry's gumboots were by the back door. After he popped them I wore them, usually with thick socks so they fit. Took me ages to get the fish smell out of them — baking soda, Chemico,

Jeyes fluid, the sun — never thought I would, then suddenly, one day, it had gone. Barefoot inside them I slipped about a bit. Got my raincoat on over my nightie and went out past the goat and the loo block to the beach, down the sandy slipway, along in front of the houses. High tide this morning, a storm tide, so I had to walk on the pebbles where they were thrown up in a cyclone in '93 and never drawn down again. I looked in Valmai's window — there she was still in her chair, mouth open, TV a blue-gleaming blob through the salt frost on her glazing.

Along the beach it got louder — 'Oy Joy!' Couldn't possibly be the wind, though it might be a noise come from waves forcing themselves between two rocks, slapping hard as planks of wood. Up the Maori end of the beach I stopped, by the cliffs. Thought I couldn't get any further because of the tide. But I watched the surf and saw that the draw-back was so hard, it had a real suck to it, so I could time it, run across the wet sand in Barry's boots, and climb the cliff rocks before the next wave came. That's when I lost the boots, one after the other, coming off behind me. I couldn't stop for them or it'd break over my head — I had to keep going. The wave loomed, grey as a kahawai curling above me, and I only just made it. The suck took the boots out.

Rex hasn't noticed they've gone. He's still out there going round and round on his little tractor on the lawn. There isn't a tree or a shrub or a flower on this quarter acre — they wouldn't stand a chance. With Rex and his mower I'd have to fence them in, like they were wild animals. Last spring I pushed some bulbs into the garden next door, a bach that belongs to some Aucklanders. I was a bit embarrassed when they came up — paper whites, jonquils and Earlicheer. Didn't think they would come up, really; I'd just loosened the dirt under the ngaios on the border of our sections and shoved them in, hadn't given them any care at all. I wonder if the Aucklanders know who planted them — their grandchildren picked them all. I should tell Rex that, that it was me, to see if they've already mentioned it to him, if the man did during one of their fishing conversations.

Round and round goes Rex, the name on the side of his mower flashing in the sun — 'John Deere' — round and round, his cap on backwards like he's a teenager, not a bachelor of forty.

Oy Joy.

He hasn't noticed the boots are gone.

When I was up on the rock I had one of my nerve attacks. Froze rigid and had to sit down on a really knobbly bit, which dug into my backside even though I took my coat off, folded it up and stuck it under me. Got drenched from the spray. The surf creamed and boiled around me on three sides and I must have been there for at least ten minutes, quarter of an hour, before it was thrown up at me.

It landed at my feet, legs spread, eyes staring. It must've been hit on the head trying to swim through the breakers, or maybe it had been wounded at the mouth of the bay where the rollers start. There was such a gash in it, I thought it was dead. I poked it with my big toe. Then it rolled a bit — just its head — rolled over to look at me and I looked into its bulgy eyes. I think I screamed then, but nobody would have heard me because the surf was so loud. Just as well they didn't hear me — I'd be embarrassed now and there was no reason to scream. That octopus looked at me with such love — there was love in its wet, grey eyes; it looked at me with the love of a child. And then I noticed it had a mouth, a small, round mouth with thin, black lips, full of sea-water. That octopus had been a fighter in its time — its head was covered in old scars, and it only had seven legs. I struggled up with it in my arms, waited for the next wave to suck out and ran back along the beach. Its head was heavy, its long legs dangled, I worried a bit it might wrap itself around me and trip me up. But it didn't. It must've known I was trying to help it.

Now all I've got to do is wait for the easterly to swing around and the surf to go down, then I can put it back in the sea. The river would be another place to take it — sometimes you see octopuses in the river — but I haven't got anything big enough to transport it. Besides, if any of the people over there saw me they'd think I was cracked. So it's in the bath. I carted up a couple of buckets of sea-water and tipped them over it. Don't know what Rex'll say if he sees it there. It's still alive — it looks up at me when I go in to check it, looks up at me with its lovely eyes.

Rex has turned his mower off and he's climbed up the water tank to check the level. There's been no rain for ages, but it's a big tank and I'm careful. Don't know why he worries.

'Mum!' He's calling me. 'Mum!'

I put my head out the bathroom window.

'What're you doing in there?' he asks. 'You've been in there for ages. You feeling crook?'

I shake my head.

'I'm going to have a drink with Valmai,' he says. 'See you later.' And he's climbing down the ladder quick-sticks, because I usually whine at him and suggest that a cup of tea with me would be better for his health.

In the kitchen I open a tin of sardines and feed them to the octopus one by one. While I'm doing it, perching on the lav and leaning over, dropping them in, I remember from one of Rex's school books that octopuses don't usually have mouths, they have a kind of beak. This must be a rare breed, maybe a new one none of the scientists know about. It opens its mouth obedient as a baby in a highchair, and swallows the sardines whole, because it doesn't have any teeth. When it's finished its mouth keeps moving, as if it's still hungry or trying to say something, the mouth pursing, pushing air in and out.

'Oy Joy' it says, but I'm not sure if that's it; I'm not sure that's what it's trying to say, I'm not sure at all.

Red Lolly

When I was a girl, my Papa would say to me — he was a New Zealander who met my mother here in France during the War — he would say to me, 'Stop playing to the crowd! Stop holding the floor!' he would say. 'Get back in your box.' He did not understand that, for me, to turn away from an admiring face is entirely against my nature; he could not comprehend that his idiomatic command to retreat to my box only brought into my mind a horrifying image of myself lying in my shroud, hands clasped.

So, I have played to audiences real or imagined all of my life — and it has brought me no end of pleasure. I like to imagine what thoughts go through their minds, every detail of their appreciation of me. Right now, for instance, there is a boy, outside the beach kiosk, watching me. He has two sisters flanking him, but they are younger and more interested in the twenty flavours of ice-cream brought down to Menton from

Nice, some of them so disgusting that just to read their names is enough to make one bilious: beer, licorice, mimosa.

The boy's mother has seen me now too, and she pauses in the lighting of her cigarette. It is hot today and I can see she is overdressed and bothered, and would like to be like me, stretched out on my foam-rubber pallet, entirely oiled and lying on my back in the sun. Would her breasts be as beautiful as mine, as firm to the touch, as sweetly positioned on the top of her chest? Mine are smooth with silicone, buoyant and brown. Would her stomach be like mine, sculptured stone? Would her limbs be as fleshless?

They don't have the technology yet for my neck, for my upper arms, my thighs — though it's on its way and will be available by the time my admirer requires it. Smoking now, about forty and overdue for some eye-work, she is sitting on a low brick wall on the other side of the narrow road between the beach and the row of kiosks.

And she will require the work eventually, my admirer, who is drawing in toxic smoke over there, watching me. Every woman in the world will want it, eternal youth — and if they can afford it, most will succumb. The money I've spent! From my third husband I inherited a fortune — and most of it is gone.

When I sit up the beach spins around me — the brown of the basting bodies, the gaudy towels, the bright primaries and whites of the beach umbrellas — a whirl of colour. So lightheaded am I that I must roll first to my hands and knees before gaining my feet. For seven years I have had trouble with this manoeuvre, and every time I attempt it I remember the face of the liposuction operator who damaged the nerve in my right leg. I remember his Oriental face and I imagine him watching me now, his narrow eyes heavy with remorse. What grace have

I inhibited? he asks himself. How fortunate it is that her beauty overwhelms her halting step!

A man has joined the woman now, a Saxon with close-cropped hair in a golden fuzz. He's big, like a German, like a Swede, like an Australian. Like her, he's seen a lot of harsh sun and is prematurely aged. Bulging slightly in her Lycra shirt, her bra straps cutting little valleys into her shoulders, his tired-faced wife smiles at him and offers him a drag on her cigarette and it occurs to me then — it makes my performance all the more bittersweet, the pleasure I take in it more acute — that he reminds me of my father.

Now I am promenading towards them, towards the shower by the path, my thighs slipping noiselessly past each other: they haven't touched for thirty years. Do they guess that I am fifty-five? I place each foot carefully, one in front of the other in the sand, so as not to jar my tendons, my distended knees. I would like to have some bone shaved from them, and my elbows, to bring the joints more into the line of my limbs.

For my next operation I will travel to Algeria. Surgeons in the south of France are grown reluctant to touch me, because of my little heart problem.

My feet find the concrete disc set into the sand, my hand finds the tap. I know this tap well, its little idiosyncrasies, because I'm here every day in summer — even through these August crowds. A slight jerk, the metal pipe gurgles and one drop extrudes from the showerhead. I extend my tongue and turn, so that the handsome blond brute can admire my derrière.

'Look!' It's one of his children. 'That lady's got no bum cheeks!'

The dear, sweet little family. They know not, but they will be my favourite audience of the day, for no other reason than that they are my father's countrymen. To hear their English — the thick, slightly stupid-sounding vowels, the muffled, woolly consonants: it is like a nursery rhyme from childhood, a cosy song sung by my late, lamented Papa.

'She's incredible!' comes the mother's voice as I turn back to them slowly, taking another drop on my tongue on the way through.

'Don't stare at her,' says the father.

'Why not?' says the mother. 'It's what she wants. Incredible.'

She said it again. *Incroyable*.

I turn once more, another jerk of the tap, another drop to the tongue. I don't want the water to touch my skin and ruin my carapace of oil. The boy says something — I don't catch it. It's earnest, serious, querying, like Jacques Cousteau or whatshisname, David Attenborough. Perhaps he is asking his mother a scientific question about how I came to be like this. The girls listen to her whispered answer too, their mouths full of icecream. Children generally like my hair, which is a pure blonde, tied in a high, smooth bun on top of my head, my blue bandanna a moat to its castle. Wearing it up so soon after a lift shows my stitches, but I decided this morning after close examination in a mirror that the space behind my ears would benefit from some air.

Anyway, the family won't be able to see the wounds from where they are, on the other side of the road. And the hairpiece does hide away my burnt, broken ends.

A final dart of water to slake my tongue before I begin to make my way between the bodies, back to my sponge pallet on the sand, carefully, carefully . . .

'That was lunch,' I hear the woman say, and she laughs.

My thong, my old brown favourite, flops between my legs

like a bandage. I don't enjoy the sensation and look forward to lying down. I always liked to walk slowly anyway, to give people time to appreciate me. When my beauty was more widely appreciated, I was sought after all up the Côte d'Azur, from San Remo to Saint Tropez . . .

Now, if I raise my head from my pillow, I can see the family finishing their ice-creams and the mother wiping the face of the smallest girl. They are obscured for a moment by crowds and then they come past me, towards the point, which they will not enjoy. It is thick with dog shit, which the Antipodeans seem to dislike even more than the Americans do.

The little girl has come to stand beside me. She is perhaps four years old. In the high sun her fair hair flares in a nimbus around the dark shape of her head. I would squint up at her, but my face is both chemically paralysed and surgically tight, so I cannot. My poor eyes take the full brunt of the sun. What is she doing? I don't trust her.

Head on one side, she puts her still-sticky hand deep into the pocket of her shorts and produces a glob of red sweets, jellies, all glued together. With the utmost concentration, ignoring her sister calling from a distance away, she detaches one moist oval pastille from the bunch and holds it out, briefly, over my stomach. After a moment she reconsiders and bends over me to gently insert the sweet between my lips. I can see her face now, the maternal tenderness in her blue eyes, the way her little mouth is pursed with concentration, the way she devotes herself to the impulse to sustain me. The sweet adheres to my teeth, it clamps my jaws shut. Then a second sweet is held to my mouth between the black-nailed thumb and forefinger, and the tiniest frown — or is it just the desire to frown? — shifts the pale skin of her brow. A moment passes before my little saint understands that I cannot accept another and so eats it herself, very quickly, chewing and swallowing so close to me that I can hear every pulse of liquid mastication.

'Anna!' The sister is calling again.

The child jumps up as quickly as a bird taking flight and I turn my head to watch her go in her little red sandals, her hurrying, plump legs still with a baby's shape to them.

A drop of water, a tear — I suppose that's what it is — rolls from the corner of my left eye, over the bridge of my nose and into my right. Through it the little girl blurs and jumps, taking her waiting sister's hand and hurrying with her down the concrete path towards her mother, between the high fence of the Stade Rondelli and the smooth, sunbaked rocks above the sea.

In a Language All Lips

The window is jammed. It won't open or shut, and the sun struggles to pierce the greasy glass.

As usual, when I wake she is still asleep. She sleeps through anything.

A fly rubs its paws on the bridge of her nose. One morning I entered her and she woke up only when I started moving. She is a stupid woman, but I like her red hair, white skin and lilting voice. She says she loves me.

There were tears last night. There will be tears again this morning when I wake her to ready her for her journey. I will prepare her in ways she will not know until it is too late.

She rolls over, her hair shifting on the pillow like weeds in the Sargasso Sea. Her violet eyes open and look at me. I bask in the purple light for a moment. I can't help myself. A small white hand threads itself through my chest hair, she nuzzles her moon face into my breast, and soon I feel the tears slip over my skin like silk. I turn her over, and we dampen the bed another way. Towards the end she smiles at me, fleetingly.

I smile at you because I love you. I smile at you because I don't want you to know how heavy my heart is — how I'm dreading this separation even though it's only for a few days.

But I will be home. Home in Ireland. And you will follow me there. If only it could happen as quickly and as fearlessly — this flight from living death to something I can scarcely remember. As quickly as conception, that confident leap to existence. That happens all too fast. I amaze myself. Even among this heat and misery, with no money of my own, I've held on to my resolve not to tell you. Not until we are at home. We will visit my parents in Armagh, and my angry, always angry sister in Belfast. Perhaps she is still in Belfast. Perhaps she is in another country, her red hair stinging the air in hotter streets. She talked once of going to Australia, where her eldritch voice would captivate, and her anger calcify into white turds of boredom. In my experience angry women are the most bored of anyone when they give up. If it were to happen to me, that calm, I would float in it like seaweed in a pool, different cool lengths of me fingering different depths, and too pliant for even the sea to enjoy manipulating me.

Your hand on my stomach is so heavy I can hardly breathe. It's as if you already know I am inhabited and would press it out, a pulpy mass on the sheets.

Ah, my lovely — you have seen the stupidity of the situation. I saw it flash through those lilac depths, a tiny silver fish. You are onto something.

You are wanting to take coals to Newcastle, as the English say. This is sillier. Place us in the same fireplace and one of us would refuse to burn. We would never burn together.

Your father was a fighter. I could've talked with him, hey? After the silence, the sizing up. You know what they will say afterwards — only an Arab could've done that. The paradox is that they won't know what I've really done. They will know I have killed you, and others besides, but they won't know why. Your death to me is a tool, for them an instrument they scarcely know the use of. But I will make myself clear, and will not be regarded as a fanatic. Perhaps we will lower them all to a crouch, inches away from falling to their knees.

You are out of bed, looking for your clothes, complaining once again of how filthy you are. You don't know what filth is.

I know you are looking at me. I know what you are thinking, but I have turned my back. I have never known a man with such resistance in his eyes. If it wasn't for the warmth of your hands, the beautiful things you say in a language all lips, the shift in your voice when you speak of the future — I wouldn't believe you love me.

I close the bathroom door. I don't know you well enough to piss in front of you.

I must move quickly to check your bag, make sure everything is in place. We will leave for the airport in fifteen minutes.

In the bathroom you — what? Surprised there is still no blood? Do you think I haven't noticed you haven't bled, not for eight weeks or more?

My shirt is damp from yesterday's sweat. My skin is crawling.

No matter where you are in the world you continue to do some things in the way you always have. I brush my hair in long lopes, from my scalp an orange slide to my waist. As a schoolgirl in front of the kitchen mirror I brushed my hair like this to catch the light. Now I do it to remind me of who I am. It reminds me of more than a dim reflection.

Once we were on a cliff top. The wind blew my hair into your face. You said my hair was a simoon, hot and laden with dust, a gust of Arabia in the salt air. You caught it and held it against your lips.

The walls of this room are pitted grey, made of something that used to be shiny. I dig the brush into my scalp and leave it there. I will have a pitted head. And my heart is pitted already, the bomb site of the soul.

At home my grandmother will talk to me of souls. She will talk of her immortality, then clasp my hand and tell me she is afraid of dying.

The Irish are so afraid of death, having been at close quarters to it at its most violent for so many centuries. Its familiarity has bred terror. If only it had bred contempt, then perhaps the fighting would have stopped. Contempt is a narrower emotion than fear and eventually gives way to indifference. It could become more of a torture to keep one's enemy alive.

It's quiet where you are. Have you gone? Perhaps to buy coffee, perhaps to escape me. I can never predict what you will do next.

I open the door quickly and you turn from the window, my carryall in your hand.

'I was looking for cigarettes.'

She hands them to me from her pocket.

'I have given you some money,' I tell her. 'Enough to get out, enough to get home at the other end.'

She is staring at me, tapping her hairbrush against her thigh. She wants to ask me where I got it from.

'It's here.' I touch the side pocket of the bag.

She turns away from me, picking up pins and combs from the table and twisting her hair in the English-lady way she has. There are too many ironies about her for me to take her seriously.

'I'm hungry.' She looks up at me from under those white eyelids.

'They will feed you on the plane.'
'I'm hungry now.'
'Too bad.' Now she'll cry.

But I won't. I will just pick up my bag and go through the door ahead of you. I won't even look back to see of you are following me. Just this once I will trust you to be there.

The cab stinks. Someone has vomited here in the early hours of the morning. Someone drunk and despairing. The driver notices her quell a retch, and smirks.

I didn't mean to give you more life than you already have. Sometimes among all the changes, running from city to city, I have almost felt sorry for you.

This is the last time we will ride together. You and I have done rather well. But you would thank me afterwards, if you could, for this solitary flight. For the release, the ticket to a quiet place.

People will look up between the buildings and see a knife flash in the sky, a red slash in the belly of God. That will be you.

Later on dusty streets I will think of you and wonder if it is you between my toes.

My brain is clogged with hormones that make me bovine. I can't think clearly. Your face has a strange sheen to it, lilac through the brown, like the dark face of a stained-glass saint with the sun behind you.

Your neck has the feel of steamed fish, a delicate meat. I would like to bite it, but we are surrounded by sweating bodies in cars. If we were alone I would do it, and you would scream. Women like you like pain, each spin of the clock to be a rimless wheel.

I lift the coins from my pocket and pay the driver. They fall into his palm, disappear. I carry your bags, your glittering death.

I am strapped in, numbed from the long wait. I ask a hostess for water. There is dust in my mouth.

I will go home and stand in the rain, be polished by the tears of God. When the sun comes out I'll watch the limpid hills, and wait for the fiery blast, the simoon.

You will never come.

You would not survive in my country with its mad, old war, and I would never survive in yours.

Red Button

My first client this morning arrives early, which irritates me. She's already in the waiting room when I come in, which makes me hurry through the correspondence that usually occupies me for the first half hour or so. When finally I send through to reception for her, I feel as harassed as she seems to be, hurrying in on her sensible shoes, her navy skirt flapping around her thick calves.

'I've never been to see anyone like you in my life,' is her opening statement, before I even open my mouth. 'I hope this will be entirely confidential.'

'Of course,' I assure her. 'You don't even have to use your real name.'

She nods her short-haired grey head.

'But I should perhaps tell you that I do recognise you — your face is familiar.' I have to think for a moment. 'I've seen your picture in the business section of the newspaper. And on television.'

'Coral Bailey,' she supplies. 'I'm the CEO of Millennium Energy.'

'Of course you are.'

She'd used her own name to book her appointment, but I hadn't recognised it on my list.

'I want to tell you about something that happened to me. Someone I met.'

'Recently?'

'During the summer.'

'Go on, then.'

There's a silence then, during which I avert my eyes, watch the trees in the park opposite flail in the March wind.

'I always drive myself,' Coral begins slowly. 'On business trips in foreign countries I will sometimes permit a driver, but on all journeys, the one I want to tell you about included, I prefer to drive myself. I had Robert with me.'

'Robert?'

'My husband. As we headed out of town we talked a little about Samantha's baby. Robert asked me if I thought she'd be awake when we got there. I said Samantha hadn't got her into any kind of routine, so who was to know. Robert took this as a criticism of Sam, somehow, and told me to make sure I didn't cause any trouble when we got there, giving instructions or whatever.'

'Samantha is your daughter?'

'Yes. He went on about how I'd always thought that Sam was hard or tough, when she was actually soft as butter, and nothing like me. His implication was that I'm a nasty bitch.'

'Do you think so?'

'He thinks I'm — what is the word he uses? Impercipient. Impercipient to his needs and desires. He sometimes says things about the "mannish carapace" of my business clothes, asks why I won't let my hair grow a little.'

'And what do you say in response to that?' I ask her. There are only three tissues left in the box, which with some of my more tearful clients would already be little sodden mounds on the low coffee table between us. Coral doesn't seem like a crier, although her voice is cracking a little.

'I say nothing, because it would lead us nowhere,' she says firmly.

'Tell me the story, then,' I say. 'Tell me what happened.'

'It was like this: I required the Ladies. In the days I allowed Robert to drive I would sit with a bursting bladder for miles. He could never stop without plenty of warning: to lift his foot off the accelerator and apply the brake was anathema to his driving self. If I gave him a ten-minute warning he could manage it — a warning gleaned from my prior knowledge of the exact location of each convenience; something he called my mental crapper map. I expanded it on every family summer holiday. And believe me, there was a quarter of the number then, compared to now . . .

'On the Pohuehue Viaduct a Rest Area sign flashed past — you know, that little man and little woman separated by a single line — and up ahead there was the building itself in a picnic spot, a gravel scallop scooping out at the side of the road, the bushy gully high around us. I swept in, took the car up onto the grass beside a vast macrocarpa and Robert lurched forward against his seatbelt only slightly. There was a wooden table of heavy slats, a rusting Ford Cortina and two toilet blocks — an old granite one boarded up with a bird nesting in one of the small ventilation grilles high under the iron roof; and a new one with plastic walls the colour of the purest, palest urine. I remember thinking it was the colour of baby pee, which must have been because I was on my way to visit a baby.'

'Your granddaughter.'

'Yes. The building had a red plastic cap, like a piece from a child's garage set, or a Monopoly house. I told Robert I'd be back in a minute and he nodded and sighed, reclined in his seat and I knew for sure as I walked away from the car that he had closed his eyes. You can't work as hard as he does at the age of sixty-three and not spend your domestic downtime exhausted. Robert is perpetually, tediously exhausted.'

Emotionally absent husband, I note.

'The toilet, it appeared, was electronically controlled, with a wide red button and automatic locks. Just as I reached the concrete-slab porch, the door began to slide open. Someone was on her way out. I paused and turned around to wait. Robert's profile was in peaceful repose. Beside the picnic table was the Cortina which, I saw now, had grass growing up under its axle. The windows were smashed, all except the windscreen, which had a pattern of silvery cracks across it, like a cobweb.

'Then, suddenly, just as I heard a step behind me, a chicken rushed out from under the car, with a huge wild cat in hot pursuit. They vanished into the long grass and I heard the impact — jaw on feathery rump — and the giant cat's paws thudding away towards the bush gully. The alarm I felt expressed itself in my bladder, which stung and burned intolerably, so I turned around again, to pass my predecessor to the toilet. But there was no one there.

'It didn't concern me. I remember thinking I must have imagined hearing the step, and that it must have been some new sensor technology, something newly installed, that had made the door slide open. I went inside and the door slid shut after me.

'There was a woman standing beside the hand-drying unit with a tube of lipstick extended in her hand. At least I thought it was a woman, until I looked more closely and saw that it was a transvestite, one of those poor devils that haunted K Road and Fort Street before Robert's lot were elected to council and cleared them all out. She wore a green nylon dress that more closely resembled a petticoat, and huge sandals, her horny toenails long and painted orange. A small, glittery evening bag hung on a chain from her shoulder.

'"Didn't you hear me cooee?" she asked. "You in a hurry?"'

Coral does a passable imitation. I can hear the tranny's voice — soft, treacly, teasing.

'"Could put this on in the car, but the rear-vision's gone," she said, bending to the narrow strip of greasy mirror in the wall and applying the lipstick. "But if you don't mind waiting, I'll just be a tick."'

'"Your car?" I said. I depressed the button on the wall, a red one to match the control on the other side, by now so desperate to pee I decided to go outside in the grass. Nothing happened. While she talked on I pressed the button at least twenty more times.

'"My mother's. On my way up north with it. She died and I'm taking it to my sister. Liar liar pants on fire! Stole it off a man I had in Albany who needed a pee as bad as you do now and left the keys in the ignition —" She paused to press her freshly coloured lips together.

'She's a nut, I realised, and the sooner I got out of there the better. I pressed the button again, to no response, only a faint whirring and clicking inside the wall, just audible under her voice.

'"Go right ahead there, girl," she said. "Don't stand there with your legs crossed." Still intent on the mirror, she dug into her shoulder bag and extracted a mascara wand.

'"Go on. Don't mind me."

'And God help me, I didn't mind her at all because I couldn't — my panties were damp and getting damper. I squeezed past and tore down my trousers and sat with a thud without even checking the seat, and it was a torrential, humiliating flow, throughout which I kept my head bowed. When I looked up at her again after I was back in order, she was dabbing on scent, watching me.

'"Feel better now?" she asked. She had real concern in her voice. It touched me in spite of myself. I felt my heart constrict with it, told her yes thank you, and went to the button again, thinking that perhaps the lock was on a timer and that now it would respond. It didn't.

'The transvestite watched me, registered my rising panic, smiling kindly. She didn't seem at all affected.

'"You've really let yourself go, haven't you, honey?" she said in the same concerned tone. She reached out then and touched me, stroked my arm, and her finger on my arm put a shiver down my spine. It wasn't revulsion because she was a transvestite, some squeamishness or fear of disease or anything, it was because I knew suddenly that she was dangerous. As she took a step closer she had an intensely predatory expression in her big hooded eyes.

'I kept pressing the button like mad, but nothing was happening. She started excavating her tiny evening bag again and lining up on the edge of the hand-basin all manner of creams, perfumes, lipsticks and eye shadows, and a packet of blue Holiday. At the time I didn't think about it, but later on, since then, I've marvelled that it could hold so much and realised that that should have been my first clue. Instead, I was calling for

Robert. I just called out once or twice, maybe three times, but there was no grille like in the old toilets, no gappy door. The Monopoly house was entirely sealed and soundproofed, and my voice ricocheted around the little room.

'"Who's Robert?" the tranny asked me, giving a bottle of nail polish a vigorous shake.

'"My husband." I remember the words were whispered.

'"He still want to fuck you?" she asked, taking a firm hold of one of my hands, the other still engaged in pushing at the wall. She was very strong — I couldn't pull it away.

'"Leave that button alone. You'll wear it out, lovie. Does he?"

'I leaned my forehead against the cool wall and immediately recoiled. It was damp, fetid with mutating microbes adhesive enough to cling to smooth plastic.

'"Does he still want to fuck you?" she asked again, squeezing my hand rather painfully as she brushed on some colour. It was bright cerise. When she realised I wasn't going to answer her no matter how hard she pulverised my knuckles, she said, "Course he doesn't. But then you don't want to fuck him any more either. Sex isn't everything, is it?"

'"Of course not," I answered her then. It was finally dawning on me that I had to talk my way out of this situation and that my previous panicked state had been due to my desperate need to pee. Now that I could think clearly I must not continue to panic. I relaxed my body, let her take the other hand, brush at the nails.

'"Love it myself," she went on. "Always been my downfall."

'I focused on the fact that she knew how to open the door. It was obvious she did, because she didn't care that it wouldn't open now. All I had to do was to get her to tell me how to get out. And if that didn't work, surely, in a few minutes, Robert would come and open it from the other side. He would wake up and realise I'd been gone for longer than it took to . . . but then again, he knew I'd had my little problem again recently, so he might leave me straining away for as long as half an hour before he came looking for me.

'Christ, what could she do to me in half an hour? I remember thinking. She could kill me!'

'Have a drink of water,' I tell her, pouring some out. 'Take a deep breath.'

Coral does both, and gets the hiccups. She gets up to walk around, rubbing her stomach.

Gastric personality type? I note.

At the window she pauses, the autumn light falling across her lined and anxious face.

'Usually I stop the story there,' she says. 'Afterwards, when I told my women friends, I stopped it there, said that the door opened miraculously and I made a lucky escape. But it's not true—' A giant hiccup cuts her off and she makes a gesture of exasperation.

'It's all right,' I tell her. 'When you're ready. Take your time.'

A few minutes pass before the hiccups slow enough for her to resume.

'I began by asking her how long she'd been stopped at the rest area. She said she'd been there a long time, she'd lost track. I tried to examine her pupils to see if she was stoned, but I didn't really know what I was looking for. I've never had anything to do with drugs, though I know they affect your internal clock, your sense of time passing. The whites of her eyes were yellow, that's all I observed.

'While my nail polish dried she smoked a cigarette, which half suffocated me in the closed atmosphere, and selected some of the make-up, making a little group of the bottles. She told me she was going to take the car on to Ruakaka and park it by the beach and sleep the night. She said she'd gone there when she was a child many times, that her tribe came from up there. I let her chatter on, but a couple of times I asked her questions like, "Was the door playing up before I came along?" and also "Where is your car parked?"

'It occurred to me that I hadn't seen it, that it must have been behind the building, concealed to me when I came in, but she wouldn't answer me. She just went on in her quiet, soothing way, smoothing make-up onto my skin, massaging my crow's feet, using a dark liner around the edges of my lips before applying the lipstick. It made me feel oddly drowsy and I had to fight the desire, after the eye shadow went on, to leave my eyes closed.

'I kept wondering when Robert would come and look for me, which distracted me from listening to her closely, and it was a while before I realised she had stopped telling me about her boyhood, but was talking about me.

'"It's hard, losing your femininity," she was saying. "Women like you get to a stage in their lives when it's easier to be male than female. Look at you — not a lick of paint when you came in, that horrible suit, those dreary shoes, ghastly haircut. No perfume, no jewellery except for your hand-crafted brooch. You're a tragic case. D'you still turn it up? You don't need to answer that, love, not if you don't want to. I'm presuming you still give Robert a hand if he asks you. It's important for a man. Use it or lose it, that's what I tell my older men friends. Some of them require more of a pumping motion than a stroking one, if you get my meaning, though you can do both at the same time if you're clever. Famous for it, I am."

'On and on and on she went! I can't remember all of it; most of it was inutterably vile. I wanted her to stop but I couldn't move. There was something in the make-up, maybe — some chemical I was absorbing through the skin that paralysed me. I couldn't fight her off.'

Coral is back on the sofa, picking up one of the cushions, laying it across her lap, picking it up again, holding it tight against her. Her cheeks are flushed.

'Then?'

'I let her . . . I —' She gulps, stops.

'You let her what?'

'Touch me. You know, she — when she'd finished making me up, she said it was time to play with the old red button and I thought she meant she was going to open . . . but she meant . . .'

Tears are close to the surface, perhaps. I push the box of tissues closer to her.

'It was so intense — I've never experienced anything like it. She had me against the wall, she had her hand . . . her hands . . . and I . . . I must have blacked out.'

'Fainted?'

'The next thing I remember was opening my eyes to the sunlight streaming through the open door and Robert standing there with an expression of horror on his face and me realising I was spread-eagled on the floor with my knickers around my ankles. He helped me up — he thought I'd had a stroke or something, a heart attack. I asked him where she'd gone, and he said "Who do you mean, there's nobody else here." He'd fallen deeply asleep for over an hour before he'd got out of the car and come looking for me. The door was standing open and there I was. He said I must have taken a turn and passed out while I was sitting on the loo. He put his arm around me and we went outside.'

Coral is quiet, breathing evenly, her eyes fixed on her glass of water, though she doesn't move to pick it up.

'And drove off?'

'Yes. But before that, on the way to our car, I saw her again. She was sitting in the front seat of the Cortina. I could only just make her out through the streaming cracks in the windscreen, but she leaned in close to the side window to give me the thumbs up and a lascivious wink as we passed by. I clung to Robert, pointed — "There she is" — and he peered in that direction, but he couldn't see her.'

'Why not, do you think?'

'Because his eyes are hopeless. Worse than mine.'

'But that wasn't the end of the story, was it?' I prompt gently, because of course I've heard the story before, from other women travellers. 'What happened when you looked in the mirror?'

'The mirror?'

'Yes. Didn't you flick down the little mirror on the passenger side when you got into the car? Because you let your husband drive then, your knees were so weak?'

'That's right. That's right. And I checked my nails, too. And it had all gone, all the make-up. Though I have, since then, you know, gone out and bought some eyeliner and mascara and nail polish — oh!' And now that she's got to the end of her story, Coral allows herself to weep. Two giant tears streak her face in perfect simultaneity.

'I'll look into it,' I promise her.

In the afternoon I contact the tohunga and the priest. Tomorrow we'll drive to the viaduct again, light some more candles, say some more prayers. It might not work, of course — it hasn't worked so far. This particular ghost is one with a mission she's not giving up on easily. Perhaps I should suggest she move to Wellington, find a public toilet near the Beehive: she'd find some likely customers there.

Striker Lolls

As soon as they're alone, as soon as Phil takes him out to see the boat, she puts her hand on Glennis's arm and says, 'What do you think of him? What do you think of Mal?'

The arm under Kirsty's hand is hard, speckled like warm sand. Glennis lifts her hands from the white foam, startled, then replaces them. Below the surface her fingers connect with a fork. It passes, steaming, in front of Kirsty and drops into the draining tray.

'He's . . .' Glennis turns to Kirsty. Her gaze drops to the tea-towel Kirsty has just picked up. Kirsty wonders if Glennis wants her to help. There's no 'thank you', or anything. Now Glennis's eyes are resting on the mosquito bite inflaming Kirsty's right thumb. Kirsty licks a finger and rubs at it, as if it is a smudge.

'He's nice, isn't he?' Kirsty says, hoping she sounds less urgent. It seems important, suddenly, what Glennis thinks of her husband.

'We should light a coil,' says Glennis, laying a wet, pink finger on the bite. 'They must like you.'

Kirsty nods and dries a plate. Outside, the men shift an oar inside the aluminium dinghy. It booms faintly, lower than their voices. Or Mal's voice. To Kirsty it sounds like Mal's voice, solo, too soft for her to hear what he's saying.

'I couldn't believe it today, eh,' Kirsty says to Glennis. 'It was amazing. Looking through the bread rack and there you were.'

'I was surprised you recognised me,' says Glennis.

'You've got the same haircut.' Kirsty fights down the urge to touch Glennis's hair. It's rich, gleaming, healthy. It reminds Kirsty of the ceilings in one of the rooms in one of the many flats they've lived in in Auckland, a varnished kauri ceiling. It looks impenetrable. She lifts a hand, then lowers it. Mal used to tell her not to touch people all the time. They don't like it, he used to say. You've got to judge people better.

Glennis laughs in a short, embarrassed sort of way, before attacking the barbecue grill. Kirsty has never seen anyone wash a barbecue grill before. Everything in Glennis's bach is lovely and clean.

'I'm sure I haven't,' Glennis says, shaking her head. 'Not the same haircut as when I was fourteen.'

'Sixteen,' corrects Kirsty. 'We were sixteen, the last time we saw each other. Remember? On Queen Street one Friday night, outside Mainstreet, when Mainstreet was still there.'

Glennis colours. Seeing the pink blush in her cheeks, Kirsty wonders at it. It's as if Glennis is ashamed of something, but Kirsty remembers Glennis as always so perfect, clever and together. She was cool.

'Where do the cups go?'

'Up there.'

In the ranchsliders the women's reflections work in the reflected kitchen. The round peaks of Glennis's shoulders gleam as she reaches from bench to sink. Across their middles, at sink level, the real world intrudes as pale waves curling on the beach. The moon is rising above the island in the bay. It sits in the fruit bowl on top of the fridge in the glass of the doors. Glennis sighs and wrings out the cloth.

'The kids were so excited, eh?' Kirsty is worried by the sigh. But perhaps it was satisfaction at seeing the job almost done. 'When I put them to bed? They just couldn't believe it. To be staying at a bach like this with the sea right there and everything. You're so lucky.'

'My parents bought the bach when I was eight, twenty-six years ago,' Glennis says stiffly. She seems embarrassed again.

'Oh no — look, I didn't mean to make you feel — I just meant that this is so *wonderful*! You know, to have met up with you again —' Glennis is looking at her arm. Kirsty's hand is on it once more. 'Sorry.'

The bach door bangs and the men come in. They stand just inside. Mal grins.

'Well,' Kirsty says to him, 'did you have a nice chat?' Mal looks the happiest he's looked for ages. 'Mal loves boats,' Kirsty tells Glennis.

'I'll make a cup of tea,' says Phil.

'I've nearly finished here,' says Glennis, in a warning kind of voice.

She must like the kitchen to herself, Kirsty thinks, putting down the tea-towel.

'I don't know about you,' Glennis is talking to the inside of the pot cupboard, 'but I've had a hell of a year, so I'm treating my time here as a real holiday for myself, which means going to bed early.' She sits up on her haunches and looks at Kirsty. 'We don't go to bed late.'

'Which means,' says Phil, 'we don't drink.'

'Oh,' says Kirsty. 'Have you got a drinking problem?'

'Of course not,' says Glennis, pink again, vigorously wiping the bench. 'Phil just means we don't sit up drinking for the sake of it. We sometimes have wine with dinner.'

'Mal used to drink,' says Kirsty. 'When I first met him. Beer and Bacardi. Gallons of it. And smoke heaps of dope. Pills, too. Anything, eh Mal?'

Mal grins again.

'Not any more, though,' continues Kirsty. 'Not a drop for three years.' Proudly she puts an arm around him. Mal looks at the ground like a man modestly receiving an award. Phil and Glennis don't smile or congratulate him, though. They just look quickly at each other and it makes Kirsty sad. Perhaps they're nervous about us, she thinks. Perhaps they are wishing they hadn't invited us back.

'What stopped you, then?' Phil is filling the kettle. 'What stopped you drinking?'

Mal's smile fades and he looks at Kirsty.

'I s'pose it was the accident,' she says. 'The car accident. He ended up in hospital for ten months.'

'See?' says Mal. He turns his head for them to see the scar, pink and rubbery, which extends from behind his ear, across his temple and disappears into his hair.

'It's so bloody hot in here,' says Glennis, striding past and screeching open the ranchsliders. A sea breeze slithers in and lifts bits of paper pinned to the noticeboard. The tinsel on the Christmas tree flickers and shifts.

'There's a wind coming up,' says Phil, following Glennis.

'An easterly.'

'Onshore,' says Glennis. 'You can still go fishing in the morning, if it doesn't swing around.'

'Mal likes fishing,' says Kirsty.

The kettle boils.

'Tea,' says Phil, heading back to the kitchen.

'Can I give you a hand?' says Kirsty. Mal pats her on the bottom as she leaves him, and sits down on the couch. Kirsty keeps an eye on him as she gets the cups, knowing that there is a way of sitting that is Mal's and no one else's — his back hunched, the feet splayed, the knees angling towards one another and his big hands clasped loosely between his thighs like a swingbridge.

'Excuse me,' says Phil.

'I've already got the cups.' Kirsty shows him, the mugs lined up along the bench.

'They're not the ones . . .' begins Phil, then decides not to worry. He gets the milk from the fridge.

'The children were really excited,' Kirsty tells him. 'Caleb was bouncing up and down. He wants to go swimming first thing.'

'How old is Caleb?'

Kirsty has already told Phil this, when they met in the shop, but of course he's forgotten. It's always like that with people who don't have children of their own.

'Just turned three. And Rosie is nearly two. They're quite close together in age, but not in personality. Rosie —'

'They must get very unsettled with all this moving around.' Glennis is standing by the table. On it she has placed a bell. It's a ship's bell, old, brass, rotund. On one side is a paler, distorted patch that is Glennis's grimly reflected face. She shakes the

Brasso and eyes the smudged, dented surface.

'This has to be done every time we come up,' she says. The cloth rubs and squeaks.

The rhythm of the bell polishing gets Mal humming. He picks up an old *Listener* and flicks through it, giving out a monotone, sounded breath. The humming started when he came out of the hospital. Kirsty doesn't notice it any more, although it got on her nerves at first. She used to tell herself, as a kind of joke, to cheer herself up, that as a legacy of his years spent roadie-ing for punk bands he'd never known any songs with tunes.

Phil hands Glennis her tea and she straightens up to take it. They both stare at Mal as he takes his cup from Kirsty. Suddenly Kirsty sees him through their eyes — his hair set with sweat and grime into feathers, the dark shadows of dirt on his face, his teeth like old hotel windows with the blinds half down. Mal gazes back at them and smiles uncertainly. Glennis blushes.

'You doing the bell, Glennis?' says Phil.

Glennis bends back to her task. 'Yes. Has to be done.' Her voice comes in forced little puffs with each rub of the cloth.

'Where did the bell come from?' asks Kirsty, putting her hand on Mal's shoulder for comfort.

'My sister's got a little bell,' says Mal suddenly. 'It's white china with tiny roses. It used to be Gran's. Gran never let us touch it. She kept it on her dressing table beside her hairbrush. My sister used to pick it up and we'd find long grey hairs wound round and round the ding-dong bit, in the middle. Once my sister rang me in Dunedin, years after Gran died, to tell me she'd found another one.'

Kirsty loves it when Mal speaks like that. It's as if somewhere inside him a damp, heavy curtain falls aside to reveal a memory never before recounted, the colours moistened and brightened by the clearing fog of his mind. They're like hothouse flowers, those memories, their genesis is so brief. Just the other day she was thinking, on the Brynderwyns, of how she should write them down. They won't be remembered again.

'Well, *this* bell,' says Glennis, blushing, 'was found in a junk shop by my sister-in-law. No family history here.' The striker lolls, like a dull tongue.

'Lovely tea, Phil,' says Kirsty.

'So,' says Phil, sitting opposite Mal, 'where were you last night?'

Mal looks blank.

'Kerikeri,' says Kirsty.

'Where'd you stay there?'

'Oh, in the car. We're camping. Mal and I have got a mattress in the back and the kids are still little enough to top and tail in the front. We put all our stuff under the car for the night and hope for the best. You know — hope no one steals it or anything.'

Glennis has stopped polishing the bell. Her hand holds the fluffy yellow cloth aloft, like a puppet. She's frowning softly.

'It's quite nice in Kerikeri. We parked by the Stone Store, near the bridge. The kids saw ducks in the morning.' Kirsty knows she's prattling. She bites her lip to stop herself.

But Mal is remembering now. He's remembering Rosie's soft, sleep-creased face appearing over the back of the seat, alight with wonder at the ducks, her little plump finger pointing, 'Bird!' He'd got up, unkinked himself from the uncomfortable bed and found some bread. Watching her feed the ducks, he'd thought his heart would burst.

Glennis puts her hand inside the bell to still the striker and wipes the top of the dome with emphasis.

'Amazing how dirty it gets in here, just from hanging on the wall.' The bell gives out a muffled dong as she rolls it over. On the beach a bigger wave hisses up on the incoming tide. Kirsty takes Mal's cup.

'Come on, love. Bedtime.' Mal stands obediently. 'Thank you for having us,' Kirsty says to Glennis. Phil is behind the newspaper.

'Are you on some kind of benefit?' he asks suddenly, lowering it.

'Yes,' says Kirsty. 'Sickness. Since the accident.'

'Just wondered.' Phil retreats behind the paper again.

'If you'd like a shower,' says Glennis, replenishing the rag with Brasso, 'there are clean towels in the bathroom.'

'In the morning we'll go for a swim,' says Kirsty, taking Mal's hand. 'Goodnight.'

Outside the night is clear and sparkling. They have a pee behind the boat and Kirsty looks at the stars. The sign of the Pot is the brightest. It's the only one Kirsty knows. Mal used to know the Southern Cross. Kirsty can never find it. Mal's piss hits the ground in a steady stream. 'Have you been saving that up all day?' she asks him.

Mal giggles. 'All that tea!'

The sleep-out has a thick, heavy smell of children asleep. Caleb is hanging half off his bunk. Kirsty settles him in again, his thin brown limbs offering no resistance. He mutters something and turns his face to the wall. In the bunk below, Rosie has buried herself in a mound of blankets. Her round, curly head, when Kirsty finds it, is damp with sweat.

'D'you think I should change Rosie's nappy?' Kirsty whispers at Mal, turning in the dark to find him. But he's begun to snore, his jandals kicked off and his clothes still on. Even in sleep his face is different to how it used to be, slacker somehow, the mouth fuller, the skin around his eyes like tissue paper. He complains to her sometimes of a terrible pain in his head. It almost comes to anger, his response to it. These days he's never angry with her, or the kids. Just himself. Rage leaps up like a huge, blind fish from a sea of bewilderment.

One of Rosie's fists, curled like a seashell, rests on the pillow. Kirsty brushes her lips against it, tastes the salt from yet another fish and chip dinner, the plastic smell of the car seats, a trace of Mal picked up from his frequent embraces.

Undressing in the dark Kirsty hopes, as she always does, for instant sleep. Then, with her arm across Mal's chest, she knows, as she always does, that it won't come for hours. She wonders what Phil and Glennis are doing. Talking, perhaps, about them. Perhaps Phil has gone to bed and Glennis is still up, cleaning something else. Kirsty wishes she and Glennis were still friends. Then she could go inside and chat, pour her heart out about Mal.

But they were never really friends. They were just in the same year at school. Glennis had been a bright star at the centre of a constellation of cool girls. Kirsty was never one of them. She'd had to accept then that Glennis was out of reach, the same as she had to now. In that way, at least, nothing had changed. Everything else had. In those days Kirsty dreamed of drifting around India in a batik skirt, stoned out of her mind. Or of working in a pub in London, wooed by a famous poet. Or of picking oranges in Cuba, fuelling the revolution. Maybe she'd also dreamt briefly about a husband and kids, but a husband who fascinated and provided, and happy, robust kids. She wished it was true, what she'd told Phil inside, about Caleb being excited. At bedtime he'd looked at her, eye level from the top bunk, and said quietly, with conviction, 'I don't like this place.'

In the morning, after their swim, Kirsty decides, they'll pack the car and leave. Mal will want to, too. A vague kind of pride moves him sometimes. Sitting beside her as she drives, he feels as though they are going somewhere, achieving something. He rarely asks the destination and if he did Kirsty wouldn't be able to tell him. The next bank, perhaps, to withdraw some money to fill the car with petrol. An orchard to buy the kids some fruit. Somewhere to park for the night.

Mal's snoring halts suddenly and in the absence of breath that follows a terrible desire wells in Kirsty's heart. Would she want that? To be left without him?

Maybe she'd find a little place somewhere, an old bach like this one, and settle in with the kids. Maybe she'd make things, pottery and clothes, and sell them to the summer crowds. She'd . . .

But Mal breathes again, deeply. Red, oxygenated blood surges through his veins. Kirsty rubs her face against his shoulder. She brings his heavy, sleeping hand to her face and kisses it as she kissed Rosie's. The coarse hair tickles her nose. She feels chilled, exhausted. It's not the travelling or the kids, but the having to be alert the whole time, having to look out for signs from Mal that he's returning. Or slipping further away.

Through the uncurtained windows some clouds slide in front of the full moon. In his dark, dreamless depths Mal rolls over, pulling her arm with him. Before the accident he'd sense when she was sleepless and wake to talk to her.

'What are you thinking about?' he'd ask.

Now he lies departed, his barrel chest thudding under her arm with a dull beat. At last Kirsty drifts, and dreams of Glennis's bell. Lolling in the polished hollow, in place of the striker, is Mal's tongue, a dolorous stem of mute flesh, moist and torpid. Above the bell, Glennis's hair swings and swells, like a bright, luffing sail.

Race

Through the plate-glass window of the Tepid Baths crèche, Thomas watched his mother, parallel to him on the mezzanine floor above the pool. Her mouth was open, she was breathing hard. Her brightly coloured thighs pumped fast above the pedals below her outstretched arms. The hands that gripped the handlebars had white knuckles. Her golden ring flashed at him, like a headlight.

It's a funny sort of bike, thought Thomas. It doesn't go anywhere. He wished it could. But if it could, where would it go? If it suddenly took off, his mother would go flying through the air above the pool of shining heads, foaming arms and legs. If she executed a wide arc mid-air she could fly through the door of the crèche, as long as it was open.

Thomas had passed through the world out there, just before this and at many other times, quickly, holding fast to his mother's hand. In her other arm she'd gripped the bundle that was his baby sister. Once or twice, as they'd climbed the stairs beside the pool to the crèche, his mother's nylon bag had bumped against his head as it swung from her shoulder. It didn't hurt — it was soft, probably her towel. Once or twice on the stairs on other visits he'd been collected by the end that carried the shampoo and moisturiser, her white-soled shoes.

When they came in the lady in the crèche had been sitting on a low sofa, reading a story to some children. Thomas's mother pushed him forward, laid Sinead in a cot and disappeared. Thomas had gone to stand on a low ledge below the window, to watch out for her.

A man got out of the pool at the far end. Thomas supposed he was a man. He could be a monkey. His front and back gleamed with wet fur, right down to his black togs. His legs were furry, too. The monkey opened a door in the white wall. A puff of steam wafted out and he vanished through it. Thomas couldn't be sure, but he might have seen a long tail slash through the mist with the closing door.

His mother was still on the bike. Her eyes were burning, fixed on a point on the other side of the mezzanine. Thomas banged on the window. She looked grim; there was something wrong.

'Mum!' His fist banged harder, without even trying.

'Stop that now!' said the crèche lady. 'Come and play with the blocks.'

Thomas allowed himself to be led away to a low table, hillocky with Lego.

Before Sinead was born, before Mum got a big tummy even, she used to put his buggy in the car, the three-wheeled speedster with the slung canvas seat and plastic bubble for if it rained. They'd drive down to the waterfront, park where there were sometimes trains and always lots of cars, the sea on one side, railway line and then the little white church on the other, and she'd run as if someone was chasing her, pushing him before her. He'd hear her soft, rapid rubber tread; the wind would rush in his ears. In winter he wore a red beanie, in summer a peaked cap and little round sunglasses. The footbridge would fly overhead, they'd pass the men fishing on the bridge, the lady in the strawberry van, the boats for sale, the yard where the canoes were. Mum's pace never varied — steady, swift.

Sometimes there was a big canoe pulled up on the first beach, with a beautiful neck like a sea dragon. If the tide was out, Mum would run him by it on the sand, and once — just once — she had stopped and let him get out from under all the straps and the little roof and plod around. He remembered it now, the hard, shelly sand, the smell of salt and seaweed and something else that reminded him of nappies; not that he wore them any more.

At the pool crèche Lego table was a boy holding a red block in his hand, shiny and big. He was a brown boy, with gleaming black hair and sharp brown eyes that bored into Thomas. He was smiling, though.

When they'd stopped at the canoe, which was just before Mum's tummy popped completely through the gap between her yellow shiny top and black shiny bottoms, there were grown-up brown people. Where Thomas lived, all the people going in and out of the big houses were pink like him. One of the men by the canoe had picked him up, so that he could see all the wooden seats inside and the paddles laid up along the sides. It seemed that the man had drawn all over his face with greeny-black felt-tip and Thomas had found that more interesting than the canoe; he'd stretched out his finger and traced along the spiral on the man's cheek. Mum had said

'Thomas' warningly, as if he was doing something naughty. The man didn't think so. He'd laughed and put him down and patted him on his head.

After that Mum had put him back in the buggy and they'd raced along to Mission Bay, where sometimes he was allowed to have a swing. In the buggy, cars rushed past in a straight line, flashes of coloured metal and glass. On the swing, the world went up and down, up and down. The tops of the tall trees jumped into the sky, the island called Rangitoto on the other side of the sea slipped and dipped. Sometimes he was glad of the chance to feel his feet on solid ground and have a little walk about, but his mother was always keen to run back to the car and get home to the phone.

He beckoned now to the brown boy at the Lego table, the way grown-ups did when they wanted to show him something, and together they went over to the painting table. He selected a brush and dipped it into the green paint. It wasn't the right kind of green — it was too bright and thick, as thick as the porridge he had at Gran's house. The boy didn't seem to mind the feel of it on his skin; he stood very still while Thomas did a spiral on his cheek and a line down the centre of his nose. Thomas could hear his breathing, soft and sweet, the faint flutter of a bogie just inside his nostril. When he closed his eyes to the brush, Thomas seized the moment and dabbed two green blobs on the boy's eyelids.

The boy remained motionless, like a doll. Thomas carried the brush over to a desk by the door, where there was a big book lying open. He'd only had time to make one wide, gloopy streak before the lady came over and took him by the arm.

'Don't do that, naughty boy. What's your name?' she asked him. 'Your mother hasn't signed you in.'

Thomas, thought Thomas, but he didn't say it. Didn't she remember him? He remembered her. The lady at the mall crèche never remembered him either, but the lady at daycare did. This lady had big, red lips and hard, strong fingers.

Behind them there was a wail and Thomas turned just enough to take in the spectacle of his ruined work: the green, smeared whirl over the boy's cheeks, the offending hands writhing at his eyes.

Maybe his name was in the book. He found a P, but his name began with a T. He lifted his face to begin explaining that he didn't think his name was there, but he couldn't be sure — because there was a T there, but it was in the middle of the word, not at the beginning of it — but the lady had hurried away to lead the boy to the handbasin on the far wall, where she wiped him up with wet paper. The paint had got into the boy's eyes and he was yowling.

His mother was gone from the stuck bike and was instead coming out of a door at the back of the pool, changed into her togs with her long blonde hair tied back in a ponytail. At the edge of the pool she turned and went backwards down some metal steps, lowered herself into the water and stretched the funny pair of bulgy eyes over the front of her face. She pushed off, staying underwater for ages, then she surfaced, swimming towards him.

Why wasn't he there too? For a moment he'd thought he was — he had felt the water rise up his thighs, warm over his shoulders. Why wasn't he down there, in the pool with his mother? He pressed his nose and lips against the glass, pushed the flat of his hands as hard as he could. His forehead wanted to press on the glass too, so he let it. Bang, bang, bang.

The boy had run to stand beside him just as Thomas's mother flipped upside down, vanished underwater and reappeared to swim away again. Thomas gazed at the boy, whose closer eye had a bead of green paint glistening on an eyelash. A faint pulse of green sheened his beige cheeks. The boy was watching someone walking below them, along the side of the pool. It was a lady with her clothes back on, with her towel wrapped up and in her bag. Her wet hair dripped thin, straight and dark into the collar of her pink shirt. She was just like Doctor Xu Xian, who gave Thomas injections and looked in his ears. Looking up towards them now, she smiled and waved before she passed out of sight to come up the stairs.

Thomas leaned in closer to the boy and imagined him still painted, the way he'd made him look before, only better. It was all wrong, he could see now. The boy's eyes were all wrong.

Then the boy was running over to where the crèche lady was talking to the boy's mother — Thomas heard her say 'green paint' and saw the mother turn to look at him. She was smiling again, shrugging her narrow shoulders and signing her name in the big book while the still slightly green boy was hugging her legs and rubbing his face on her trousers.

Thomas's mother said she was sorry to the crèche lady for forgetting to sign him in, and then asked if it would be all right if she sat down to give Sinead a bottle. He snuggled in beside her on the low couch, breathing in the smell of the pool still on her skin, the smell of Sinead's milk. His eyelids felt heavy and downwards-drifting and he slept for a little while, dreaming of the boat-studded sea by the dragon. His mother pushed him along in his buggy — only it wasn't his buggy, it was the stuck bike, which could work now — and he was on the handlebars, racing past the sea, which was foaming with swimmers who all lifted their carved, whorled faces to watch him go by.

My Private Joy, My Comfort

Last Monday my friend Lloyd took me out to dinner. I got there early, to make sure we had a smoker's table. Lloyd's a bit slack on that side of things: he's organisationally impaired. I'd gone to Glengarry's earlier in the day to get some wine — I was really looking forward to it, I'd been looking forward to it for days.

Had a bath at six, a quiet drink on my own before I left the house. Lloyd had said a fortnight before, 'Come out for dinner. My shout!' He hadn't mentioned Fran.

So I was a tiny bit annoyed when I saw her swanning through the restaurant door, closely followed by the tall, slender shape of Lloyd. They'd come together. And I thought, of course — with his other wives he'd got out more; he could keep his women friends apart. Fran and I had met up only occasionally. Now that he's married young Melissa, he has to put us together. She doesn't let him out much. It's happened a lot in the last year or so: nearly every time I've seen him Fran's either been there or come later. I should have expected it.

'Lloyd!' and I jumped up brightly, sparkling, flung my fag into the ashtray and squeezed his arm. Lloyd is a true Pakeha of his generation, not big on kissing in public. Or in private, come to think of it, with me at least. I often end up squeezing his arm.

Fran looked at me quickly, and away, hooking her fake fur over the back of her chair, her red mouth already open and prattling on about getting the wine opened. Lloyd sat down before either of us, unsheathing two bottles from their paper condoms. It's not an original image, I know, wine bag as condom, but I remember I thought of it as the bags whizzed off and Lloyd plonked the bottles on the table. It was apt for what transpired: a large skeleton, with its pants down, fell out of a wardrobe. Nothing will ever be the same again.

'How's Melissa?' I asked then, Fran and I both sitting down, looking at Lloyd.

'Fine. Blooming!' said Lloyd. He looked great himself. I have to remind myself Lloyd's in his mid-forties. He looks about ten years younger with his healthy, taut skin, the grey negligible in his glossy black hair. And his lovely brown eyes: warm, happy, sane.

'You look wonderful,' Lloyd told me, kindly. I didn't, of course. Great bags under my eyes, my face improving on its sultana imitation every day.

'So do you, Fran,' I said, completing the circle. Fran pursed her lips together and flashed a look at Lloyd as if to say, 'We know she's bullshitting.'

The waiter brandished the corkscrew.

'Thank fucking Christ!' shouted Fran. 'I was nearly fucking dead of thirst!' She thrust the bottle at the waiter and stuck her tongue out, panting like a dog. The waiter, a bemused and gentlemanly Thai, smiled benignly, his eyes resting momentarily on her moist, flopping appendage.

Fran always swears.

While the waiter poured out for Lloyd, Fran said quietly to me, so that Lloyd wouldn't hear, '*We* didn't have a drink before *we* left home.'

'Neither did *I*,' I said, hating her. Could she smell it on my breath?

But I was blushing. There's a theory that people who blush are fundamentally dishonest. I think the opposite is true — we blush in the face of insincerity. Blushers are people who can very quickly discern the real meaning of a mean-spirited remark.

In this case it seemed I was wrong. Fran went on to say, conspiratorially, 'Melissa wouldn't let us.' Her eyebrows were waggling. Lloyd raised his glass to propose a toast.

'To what?' he asked.

I couldn't suggest anything because I was still trying to interpret those eyebrows. Fran erupted suddenly with a loud bark, startling me.

'What a question!' she shouted. 'What a fucking question!'

Lloyd bobbed his head, twisted his glass a quarter turn and took a sip. Fran obviously knew something I didn't.

'"To what?" he fucking says. As if we could fucking toast to anything else! This is a big one, Lloydie, this is really fucking big.' She was laying it on so thickly with the expletives that I wondered if she was building up to one of her sudden rages. But she was grinning, excited.

Melissa is pregnant. Having spawned itself in my stomach, the truth travelled onion-flavoured like an anaesthetic up my spine: *Lloyd is having his inevitable late child.* The stomach-voice reminded me how inevitable it was: he was an attractive man, young women found him attractive, young women often wanted to have babies. We'd never see him alone now. Melissa would be always there — she wouldn't let him get away with as much as the ex-wife, the woman who had had his sons. It was as if Melissa was here now, suddenly, curled up against him like a pale, crop-haired cat, her green eyes creased with contentment in her silent, unnerving Madonna face.

'Oh!' Fran took a sudden, scouring breath as she lit a cigarette. 'I've just realised! Bridgie doesn't know! She doesn't fucking know!' She clamped a heavy hand on my shoulder. 'Or does she? Have you told her yet, Lloydie?'

Lloyd, meeting my eyes, seemed to suffer a sudden bolt of empathy. It was as if he only just realised, in that moment, what this news would do to me. A hand shot out, across the table, surreptitiously among the cutlery. I thought he meant to lay it over mine — I could feel the dry warmth of its palm already — but he merely tapped me twice with his index finger, above my knuckles, before withdrawing. He wasn't going to get involved with my pain.

Lloydie, I thought you were my mate.

'Well, go on, don't piss about!' shouted Fran.

'I'm going to be a father again,' Lloyd said quietly. 'Due in March.'

'Isn't it fucking wonderful?' Fran scarcely waited for him to finish. She held her glass at the full extent of her arm above her head. 'To Lloydie, Melissa and the next Little Fucking Lloydie! Got any names yet?'

'When did you find out?' I asked, in an undertone I have perfected for use around Fran.

'This morning. I went up the road and bought one of those test-kit things. Six weeks gone, we think.'

Fran was still talking. 'Glue would be a good name, don't you think? Or Gluette if it's a girl. Glue for the old relationship.'

'Pardon?' said Lloyd sharply, picking up the menu, giving it a crack. Fran gave me a bruising nudge in the ribs.

'Well, congratulations!' I found it in me at last — the heart to say it. And mean it. 'Melissa must be over the moon.'

'We both are,' Lloyd said primly.

'Is it a surprise? For you, I mean . . . did you plan . . . or did it just . . .' Too late I remembered — though how I could I have forgotten? — how much Lloyd hated those kind of questions.

'Let's order.'

He's regretting it, regretting taking us out to dinner. We're a pair of old snakes. Fran, realising she'd overstepped Lloyd's considerable bounds of decency, had her lips firmly pursed together and was studying the menu.

'Mixed entrée? Tod man pla and spring rolls and money bags and all that?' she suggested soothingly. Poor Lloyd, I could hear her thinking, Bridget could at least pretend to be pleased for him.

'Good idea,' said Lloyd as the waiter loomed.

We talked about other things then. Through two and a half bottles of wine, the entrée and the main course — all of which were delicious — we talked about Fran's difficult flatmate, whether or not Fran and I should get dogs, and how long it was since Fran had last gone out to dinner. We talked about Lloyd's stressful job, his house renovations, a holiday he and Melissa had planned. Then, as he spooned up the last fiery morsels of Crying Tiger and Waterfall Beef, more relaxed now with two-thirds of a bottle of wine inside him, he asked, 'And how about you, Bridgie? How's your garden?'

I'm not talking about my garden, not in front of Fran. It's pathetic.

Is that all I have to talk about? That and my part-time job in Lloyd's brother's video shop.

'It's winter,' I offered. 'The garden's a sea of mud.'

'Melissa has huge respect for you as a gardener,' Lloyd said magnanimously. 'She's learnt a lot from you.'

The day I first met Melissa I gave her a whole lot of baby plants from my succulents bed.

It's famous, in a small way, among our friends, my succulent garden. I've been collecting them for years. I love them: their thick, juicy protuberances, tender, tough and vulnerable. Some of them grow spikes for protection. Some of them, like the aloe, have medicinal properties. Melissa is more into that side of them than I am. She's forever dabbing their juices onto the cuts and sores of Lloyd's boys, the children from his first marriage.

'I s'pose Melissa would like a girl.'

'Doesn't care, I don't think. I would, though, I'd like a daughter.' Lloyd's voice was soft, his eyes shone.

Fran's black voile arm lurched around the table, sloshing wine into our glasses.

'Bridget Frances, or Frances Bridget?' she shouted. 'Which will it be?'

'Neither, I shouldn't think,' said Lloyd, guarded now, his famous cool.

'Shall we have coffee here, or go elsewhere?'

We went to Fran's. Her flatmate was away and, judging by his half-packed boxes, he was intending to go away forever immediately after he returned. Fran's two cats lay entwined by the heater. In the kitchen their mistress banged about with cups and coffee pot. Lloyd was leaning on the mantelpiece above the cats, staring at a photograph in a heavy, hand-wrought silver frame. He looked quizzical, worried even.

'I haven't seen that before,' I said. 'Is it a recent acquisition?'

I moved in front of him and took it down. It was a beach scene, the sea and sky tropical, the couple centre frame tanned and happy, he with his arm across her shoulders. It was Lloyd and Fran, fifteen years younger, some time in the late eighties.

'Where was that taken?' I asked Lloyd's back as he retreated to a sofa.

'When Fran and I . . . you remember . . . or perhaps you don't . . . when we went —'

Fran appeared, bearing coffee and Scotch. She thumped the tray down on a table, startling the cats.

'Let's get some of this fucking hard stuff inside us,' her voice boomed. 'With coffee. Yum, yum, fucking yum!'

My fingers felt sweaty on the silver suddenly, as if they were about to dismantle a bomb, or pick a shard of glass from a child's foot, or handle a deadly poison. I moved behind Fran's bent-over bottom as she poured out, to replace it.

'You like that picture, Lloydie?' she asked as I passed. 'That was such a happy time. Probably the best time of my —' She stopped. 'Oh no! Jesus! I'm not going to fucking say that. Then you'd know how really fucking tragic my life is!'

The frame wobbled, found its balance and I turned back to the room. Lloyd took a Scotch from Fran but put it down beside him. He was pacing himself, I noted, and realised he hadn't had a cigarette all night.

'You given up smoking, Lloyd?' I asked, in my undertone.

Fran knocked back her shot and poured herself another.

'But no — bugger it. I should be able to say that, even in front of Bitchie Bridgie. It was fucking wonderful, even the fucking was fucking wonderful!' Fran shouted. She flopped down beside Lloyd. 'In Bali. You were in Wanganui — it was when your mother died. After Liz left Lloyd. We went to Bali, eh, Lloydie? We had a fucking fantastic time.' Fran was making strange little gastric noises, somewhere between a burp and a hiccup. I'd seen her inebriated enough times to know a vomit was imminent.

Fran Vomit Stories. Everybody's got one.

Lloyd stared at the cats. 'As I recall,' he said slowly, deliberately, 'we attempted sex only once, against my better judgement, and we failed because I was too drunk.'

Fran caressing him, holding him, kissing him? Lloyd's warm hands around her waist, his sweet mouth nuzzling her enormous tits? Fran's hand cupping his balls, stroking his bum? They'd had breakfast in bed together. He'd been tender . . . with Fran?

There was an awful howl, and it took a moment for me to realise it was coming from myself. The cats fled. Lloyd shot to his feet, spilling coffee on Fran, who yowled and retched in the same instant.

'Bridgie, don't!' Lloyd's appalled face swam towards me, Fran behind him with her head between her knees.

I followed the cats. I was in the hall, through the front door, on the street, in my car, gone. Lloyd didn't follow me.

Maybe he stayed behind to clean up Fran's sick.

Maybe he gave it five minutes, then left himself.

It's Sunday today and I am weeding my succulents. Every now and then one of them gets a spike through the hole in my gloves. I've gone over and over that evening in as much detail as I possibly can. Nearly a whole week has passed and neither of them has rung me. You'd think Lloyd would. He must see that he has betrayed me and in no small way. I thought we had a contract, a kind of unspoken agreement, he and Fran and I: that he was to share his heart and mind with us, his body reserved for his wives and a few in between who didn't matter.

When I came home on Monday night, pissed and tearful, I went though my shoeboxes of photographs and there wasn't a single shot of Lloyd and me alone. Sure, lots of photos of us, but always in a crowd, different crowds, right back to 1972. I felt despairing then, all the photos spread around me.

Now I'm plugging tulip bulbs into the soil, even though it's too late. They'll rot. I should plant some sweet basil, too, because it would inevitably curl up with frostbite and die, which would be right and true and proper because I fail at everything . . .

And then suddenly, without warning, I have an unbidden hallucination, the sort usually reserved for dreams in the dark. Here he is as Fran never had him: his brown arms around me, our bodies spooning together, making love. His narrow, warm chest is against my back, the rough hair of his flanks against the underside of my thighs, his breath like kisses on the back of my neck, his wonderful dick moving inside me, his beautiful fingers between my legs . . . and it's never happened. It never will. Our impossible love is perfect, glistening, unrealised: my private joy and comfort.

I stand up and brush down my knees. Yes! It's true — and wonderful! I am Lloyd's only true platonic friend! There is a definite line and Fran stepped over it. For Lloyd there will always be the spectre of their flailing, sweating, non-consummating bodies — or maybe only in Fran's mind. I feel like dancing, right here in the mud, spinning like a kid. For Lloyd I am unique.

My love for him sparkles and flares like a jewel, precious beyond belief, and I hold it dear all the way inside to ring him up.

Menschenfresser

In two days she had to leave Litia's hotel and catch the bus back to her village. Well, they were expecting her. If she didn't show up, what then? One of her brothers would be sent to fetch her, or more likely her father. He would combine the trip with church business and sit silently retributive beside her in his dark clothes, all the way back to Londoni. If he found her as she was now, he would tell her she'd disgraced not only him, but her matagali, her village and the AOG (Assembly of God) as well.

Werner looked at her and wondered what she was thinking. He'd noticed that she was often pensive, the smooth field of her brow furrowed. He extended a fat, puce finger and ran an imaginary plough between her eyes. As he'd expected, she brushed him away like a fly. He sighed. A hard nut to crack, this one. He'd had more success with the local girls on his previous holiday in Fiji, but that was years ago and he was slimmer then. And wealthier.

The noodles hissed out of the pot into the colander. Margaret turned from the sink to the gas ring. A thin, golden beam of oil dribbled into the pot, the blue flames leaping like dogs.

'What are you doing now?' asked Werner.

'Cooking your lunch,' said Margaret.

'Not like that.'

'Yes, like this.' She dropped a handful of chopped onion and carrot into the oil and stirred it. 'You open this.'

Werner had a tin of tuna pressed into his hand.

When she said she'd cook his meal he'd got his hopes up for some island delicacy. The primitive kitchen shouldn't have hindered her. They didn't need much, these Fijian girls — a fish, some coconut milk, some dalo leaves.

Margaret used her teeth to open a packet of instant noodle mix. She sprinkled the powder over the vegetables and tossed in half a cup of water.

'Not like that!' Werner was almost shouting. Margaret flinched.

'Yes, like this,' she said, fetching the drained noodles and adding them too. Werner stood with the tin of fish still in his hand.

'Come on,' said Margaret, 'open it up.'

'What?' gaped Werner.

'The ika,' said Margaret. 'Open it up.'

She took the pot from the heat while Werner struggled with an antique tin-opener. Despite his flab, his buttocks stiffened with the effort of forcing the rusty tooth into the top of the can. Margaret laughed at him, her voice hurling against the stained walls of the hotel kitchen.

'Shut up,' said Werner.

'Shut up yourself,' said Margaret.

There were little pools of sweat in the dimples of Werner's shoulders, the odd hair standing up in them like burnt mangroves in a fleshy swamp. His faded orange singlet had dark patches of moisture on it that weren't drying in the steamy kitchen, dark patches that, when he turned around, interfered with the design on the front. It was of two pigs rutting and the words 'Makin' Bacon'. It made Margaret embarrassed, that shirt.

Werner shoved the tin at her and some of the oil slopped onto her wrist. She shook it off into the pot with the tuna, stirred it all and held the empty tin out to him.

'Ekelhaft,' said Werner, staring into the pot. It looked revolting. As he took the jagged tin he flicked it up hard. Blood welled from her soft palm.

'Aaeee!' She dropped the pot handle to cradle her hand. 'Look what you've done!'

It was only a superficial cut, Werner was sure. He took her hand tenderly and kissed the back of it before turning it around to inspect the damage. There was a gossamer flap of skin and a lot of blood, as red as his. He put his mouth to the cut and licked at it. An expression of disgust crossed Margaret's face and she pulled away. She turned on the cold tap. The water ran pink into the stone sink.

Werner served the meal. It didn't look too bad, slopped out onto the plates. Sort of Chinese and anyway, he admitted to himself, he'd eaten worse. He carried the plates out to the verandah and put them on a shady table.

'Bring the forks!' he shouted to Margaret from the corridor.

The tap was still running and he could hear Margaret speaking Fijian with an answering woman. Litia had gone to the supermarket. Who else could it be? he wondered. Another cousin?

He sat down heavily on the most reliable-looking chair. Its torn vinyl spiked his thighs, even through his blue cotton shorts. Werner grimaced, his fleshy upper lip forcing his moustache hairs into his nostrils. He sneezed hugely.

'Margaret!'

The tap was still running faintly. A mynah landed on the verandah rail and eyed the lunch.

'Verschwinde!' Werner flicked his hand at the bird. 'Margaret!' The bird flapped its wings but remained perched. Werner ate some of the noodles with his fingers. In Indian style, he told himself.

Litia came up the long steps from the road, burdened with plastic bags of fruit and vegetables. As she bowed her head with the weight, a single grey hair sparkled in the sunlight. She didn't recognise him from last time, Werner was sure. He remembered her, though. The single grey hair seemed the only indication that the thirteen years since he was last here had passed for her, just as they had for him. She looked up and smiled.

'Bula!'

'Bula,' he said, and sighed.

'You are having some lunch?' asked Litia.

'No forks!' said Werner, shrugging and turning out his hands. Litia laughed. He looked like an enormous reef fish, pink and orange and blue. She waved and went inside. The hotel had been quiet these last few days — just a few locals and not many backpackers. It gave her some time for herself, today maybe even some time with her feet up.

Margaret was coming down the corridor with two forks in one hand, the other with a rag wound around it.

'Bula,' said Margaret. She rattled the forks at Litia. 'He will be getting mad!'

But Werner wasn't mad at all. His plate was empty and Margaret's food had been carefully rearranged so that she wouldn't notice any missing.

She didn't. It was so lovely out on the verandah, the gentle, creamy breeze, the birds, the click-clack of the palm leaves, the blue of Suva Harbour through the mango leaves. Werner looked contented, leaning back, lighting a cigarette with greasy fingers. Margaret settled down at her plate and began her lunch.

'Who were you talking to in the kitchen?' asked Werner.

Margaret's eyes widened, as if startled by his question, and then narrowed. She looked shifty. Werner hadn't seen her look shifty before. It was interesting. He hadn't thought her capable of it.

'Who?' Werner repeated.

'No one.' Margaret filled her mouth with noodles and brushed an ant off her plate. 'You shut up and smoke.'

Werner smiled, in spite of himself. She could be cheeky, this one. He wondered how old she was. Eighteen? It was difficult to tell. They didn't wrinkle up the same as white women.

'Are you going to come out with me tonight?' he asked.

Margaret spoke with her mouth full. 'Where to?'

'The Townhouse Hotel. That bar on the roof. I saw it from the street this morning.'

Margaret laid a noodle on the verandah rail for the mynah. It picked it up and flicked it around its beak.

'Well?'

There was a rustle of dry leaves as a mongoose streaked out from a stand of bamboo.

'Well?' he said again.

'All right,' said Margaret. 'Vinaka.'

She smiled broadly at him. He wondered if his luck was about to change. After all, he was different from a lot of white men you see in the tropics. Scrawny, pathetic specimens most of them, wasted by the heat and prematurely withered. There was one in this hotel, a skinny, bearded New Zealander carrying on a clandestine affair with a young Indian woman from Sigatoka. Werner had noticed them together, cooking in the kitchen, doing their washing in the laundry. Alone, the woman was nervous, always looking over her shoulder, waiting to be discovered. When her lover was near she nestled into him, her face blissful.

Margaret had scarcely touched Werner. He'd felt her eyes on him though, like before, in the kitchen, when he was opening the tin. She began gathering up the dishes.

'How's your hand?' he asked.

Margaret shrugged and a rueful laugh escaped her. 'Okay.' She carried the plates down the corridor to the kitchen. Her dry feet rasped on the wooden floor.

Werner would try to remember this heat during his next German winter. There was a time when he thought he'd never experience one of those again. He was sitting pretty in Auckland, landlord of two substantial blocks of flats in Papatoetoe. The money was falling into his lap. Although Margaret didn't realise it, he'd had plenty of experience with people like her — coconuts — though most of them, as he recalled, didn't have such frizzy hair. Then his wife had started kicking up, his beautiful blonde Kiwi wife whom he'd met at Oktoberfest, and he'd lost everything in the settlement. Dale had had a better lawyer, that's all it came down to.

Where was Margaret now? Possibly making coffee — and properly, he hoped, in the way he'd taught her the day before yesterday.

The world around Margaret swam and leapt. It was like being

underwater. She spun to catch the night breeze and gentle rain on her face. Below them, the government buildings gleamed green and grey in their night lights and the rugby players ran and crashed in Albert Park, like waves on a reef. She could feel Werner's arm around her, turning her to face the hill ahead.

Margaret closed her eyes, her stomach aching and bloated with beer. In a flash she saw Werner's mouth bending to her bleeding palm, his pale tongue licking. There was a story, a story she remembered an old auntie telling her at home in the village. It was about a German, a German like Werner, fat and white, who'd found himself washed ashore near Londoni. Margaret's auntie had heard the story from her auntie.

Herr Beilman had become, a hundred and forty years ago, a man of hideous appetites, joining in the feasts of bakalo and kurilagi. He would go to the temple and wait among the people for the first head to loll on the killing stone. As the story had it, he preferred children and had once dined with Tanoa on his return to Bau, the mast of Tanoa's canoe festooned with the corpses of infants. A cannibal, in his own tongue a Menschenfresser . . . But after only a few months he had offended his chief host and filled an oven himself. Margaret's auntie had always allowed herself a chuckle at this point in the story.

On the steps, Werner's arm tightened. Margaret wanted to sleep. She flopped over his arm like a doll, barking her shins on the concrete.

'Eins, zwei, drei, vier . . .' Werner counted the steps for her, 'Funf, sechs, sieben . . .'

The hotel foyer was dark. Margaret wondered how Werner could have remained so sober — he'd drunk more than she had. He was guiding her down the dim corridor to her room. Behind Litia's door a radio tinkled.

'Liti —' began Margaret.

Werner put his hand over her mouth.

'Shshsh — she's tired. She's had a long day. We won't disturb her,' he whispered. 'Where's your key?'

Margaret gestured weakly at her handbag, which still clung, miraculously, to her shoulder. There was a jumbling and a jangling as Werner's fingers raked through it.

'There now.'

They were inside. He was laying her down. She closed her eyes. Werner turned the fan on and took off his thongs. Margaret looked so beautiful, her face soft, asleep. The light from the window fell on her hand, the dark shadow of the cut under her gently curved fingers. He lay down beside her and took her in his arms.

'Margaret?'

There was no response. He put his face close to hers and smelled the beer on her breath. Stupid. She hadn't had any dinner, so no wonder. He stroked one of her breasts and the nipple hardened. Werner moved himself against her.

The village Herr Beilman had lived in was now abandoned. Margaret had been there once, as a child, with a tourist who'd wanted to see it. The killing stone still stood then, surrounded by undergrowth. She hadn't liked the place, already knowing her auntie's story and other stories besides. The tourist had found some kind of thrill in it, stroking the stone and shivering.

'Margaret.'

It was Werner, pushing hard against her thigh. She forced herself to open her eyes.

'Go away,' she said succinctly.

Werner laughed. 'You don't mean that,' he said, kissing her forehead.

Margaret lifted her mouth as if to kiss him, but travelled on to his nose, his pink reef-fish beak. She fastened her teeth around it.

'Sheisse!'

Werner had his plump hands on her shoulders, forcing himself up and off the bed. Margaret's head lifted from the pillow and then she released him, her mouth full of sweat with a faint tang of blood. She rose unsteadily to her feet, the room heaving, and ran at Werner, shoving him. He was yelling, his hands over his face, yelling halting, guttural words of abuse. She shoved at him again and again, working him in stages through the door. With the last shove he struck up against the opposing wall. The key was still in the lock. She brought it around to her side of the door and fastened it closed.

After a while Werner's footsteps sloughed off down the corridor. Margaret's desire for sleep went with him. She went to the window and looked out. The wind was beginning to pick up, and the rain struck hard against the glass. Standing there with her arms hanging limply at her sides, Margaret wondered if it was raining at home. She pictured her mother's face, asleep, peaceful. There was no surge of nostalgia, or even frustration, at the thought of returning. She brought a hand to her breast and laid it there, wondering if her heart had somehow died before she had.

The night's dense rain brought with it a determined silence. Upstairs in Werner's room his heavy bulk fell into bed, the sound muffled and as tiny as a bird landing on a tin roof.

Phone Gene

'You sit there and we'll ring everybody up and see if they like you.' Portia's cigarette stuck out between her stubby fingers like a little mast on a capsizing yacht. She was actually doing the F sign, thought Hannah. Sometimes Portia did for real anyway, out car windows.

'You're giving me the finger,' she said quietly, while she sat by the phone, which was the kind that was stuck to the wall, with a curly cord. But Portia wasn't listening; she was dragging on her fag without even coughing, her eyes resting on something moving in the garden beyond the deck. Hannah saw how the blue semicircles of her irises, just the profile of them, swivelled from one side of the lawn to the other. They were focusing on her enormous dog chasing a cat, perhaps, or a bird. Hopefully it *was* Portia's dog, which would mean it was outside and not lying in wait in another room.

Extravagantly, Portia blew out smoke and turned to face her. At the brown end of the cigarette her lips looked like pale pink beads in the shape of shells.

'Now you're really making the fuck sign,' said Hannah. Portia glanced at her upraised hand.

'Look — it's like the fingers,' she said. 'Cool. All those adults out there giving the finger and they don't even know.'

'I already said that!' Hannah felt brave. 'I said that before. I saw it first. I —'

'Go and get the air freshener from the bog,' said Portia. She narrowed her eyes against the smoke. 'Mum'll be home in a minute.'

Hannah set off down the hall, which had sides of soft brown board with white splotches and babyish pictures done with felt-tip. Portia was too cool to draw on the gib board now — she was ten. She didn't let Hannah do it any more either. Hannah tried hard not to think about the dog. Thinking about him was sometimes enough to bring him to her, lolloping out of one of the doorways.

The tin of freshener was pretty, a glistening cylinder with conical flowers in every shade of purple. *Spring Grove*, it said. On the way back down the hall Hannah gave it a tryout, puffing a hazy silver cloud just ahead of her. When she walked through it some of the droplets clung to her hoodie like glitter.

In the living room Portia had stubbed out her cigarette — Hannah couldn't see where. Maybe she'd just thrown it off the deck. The sliding doors stood ajar.

'Give it here.' Portia held out her hand for the tin. All her fingernails were felt-tipped luscious red, which had seeped into the quicks. Her other hand held the walkabout phone close to her ear. 'Sit down,' she said. 'You listen on that phone.'

The first person they rang was the new girl. Portia considered that she most likely would have nothing interesting to say. She didn't know enough yet. A man answered and went off to get her.

'Hello?'

'Who was that?' asked Portia into the phone. 'Breathe more quiet,' she said to Hannah.

'My brother. I'm not breathing loud,' came Nicole's voice. You could tell Nicole was fat even from her voice. It was a fat girl's voice, which came out thick and kind of gluggy-sounding from deep in her creamy neck.

'Have you got a brother that's a man?' asked Portia. There was a sudden hollowness, as if at the other end Nicole had removed her head from the phone. Then there was a muffled bump and thump and somewhere nearby the rumble of the brother talking.

'What's she doing?' asked Hannah, forgetting for a moment that she was not supposed to say anything. Swiftly, Portia swung the portable phone behind her back, pushing it into the seat of her jeans. They were skaties jeans. Hannah wanted a pair just like them, with all her heart.

'Be quiet!' hissed Portia, like a pissed-off mother.

'Hello?' It was Nicole.

'Has your brother sexed yet?' asked Portia. 'Has he got a girlfriend?'

'No,' said Nicole. 'I don't know.'

'Are you Christian or something?'

Nicole didn't say anything then. She just breathed, more softly than Hannah did.

'Hey, um . . .' Portia sounded casual. She put one foot up on the sofa and inscribed above Hannah's head a sweeping, silvery arc of perfumed vapour. 'Do you like Hannah?' Hannah felt her heart constrict. Her fingers gripped the handpiece so hard they stung at the knuckles. She could feel the silvery mist descending.

'She's all right. She doesn't even talk to me, hardly.'

'Right.' Portia strode towards the dining alcove. On the table was the survey form she'd drawn up. 'So what do you give her out of five?'

'I don't know.'

'Two? One?'

There was a pause. 'Three,' said Nicole, carefully. Portia clicked the Talk button and marked Nicole's column with her new peach-scented orange pen.

'You didn't even say goodbye,' said Hannah.

'You dial the next one,' Portia said. 'You ring Sia.'

Hannah pushed 3. That was all she could remember. Portia rolled her eyes and finished punching in the number for her, reading it from the top of the survey form.

'Hello?' It was a little old lady. Portia could tell from the way she said hello that she probably couldn't even speak English.

'Is Sia —' began Hannah, but Portia pressed Talk and glared at her.

'Not you. I'll do the talking.' She pressed Redial. This time it was Sia's big sister, who took ages looking for her. While Portia waited, she went out onto the deck to smoke. Tethered to the wall, Hannah watched her through the glass doors. The trees in the garden drip-dripped. The cigarette in her mouth was the same one as before, bent and blackened at the end. This time it did make Portia cough, maybe because it was already a bit used up. She only had a couple of puffs before she stubbed it out carefully on the edge of a pot plant and threw it into the long grass down below.

'She's not here. She's gone down the dairy.' It was the big

sister back again.

'Shit!' said Portia, loudly. It was louder in Hannah's ear than it was through the air. As Portia came back inside she clicked the phone off. 'Ellie, now. And we'll need a new person to make up for Sia. There has to be an odd number, otherwise it won't work.' She was copying Ms Ash, their teacher, Hannah could tell. Portia put her pen up to the corner of her mouth just like Ms Ash did.

The phone hardly rang before Ellie answered it.

'What are you doing?' Portia asked.

'Playing with my new rat. I've left nine messages for you. Who've you been talking to?' There was a jealous tone in Ellie's voice. Portia felt it thrill her, up and down her spine.

'People. I'm finding something out.'

'What?'

'Do you like Hannah?'

'She stinks.'

'Blah!' Hannah couldn't help it. It just came out. 'Blah! Blah! Blah!' She banged the phone up and down in its cradle a few times and rapid-fired some buttons. 'Blah!'

'Out of five? What do you give her?' Portia was shouting.

'Zero!' shouted Ellie, just as Hannah lifted the phone to her ear again. 'She's a loner, she's a loser, she's a user.'

Hannah suddenly felt all tight around the lips. She carefully replaced the phone and went out of the room. Portia heard the gentle scrape of a schoolbag being lifted from the polished floor and the click of the front-door snib. As the door swung open, there was the soft growl of a car coming to rest in the carport.

'What's she doing there anyway?' Ellie was demanding. 'What's she doing at your place?'

'I've told you,' Portia placated, heading down the hall, 'she's only my neighbour. You're my best friend. It's different.'

'Is it just the two of you there, on your own?' asked Ellie.

'Nah. Oliver is doing his homework.' She gave her brother's bedroom door a hefty kick as she passed it. There was no response, which meant he was probably online. Through the open door at the end of the hall she could see her mother unloading groceries from the boot. She could hear the plastic of the shopping bags crackling in the wind as they were set down on the path.

In her room she lay on her bed, the phone warm in her ear while Ricky Martin gazed down from above, oblivious to the arrow sticking into his head from a blood-red smeary cloud. Ages ago Ellie had written GAY up there in lipstick and Portia's mother had tried to wipe it off.

'Mum's got a baby book to look for names for our baby,' said Ellie. 'I looked up Portia.'

'Yeah?' Portia looked at herself in the mirror and wished she had bosoms. Then she could fit real size 8 from a ladies' shop. Then she'd look just like Britney Spears.

'It means hog,' said Ellie, only just containing herself. 'A dead famous person called Shakespeare used it in a play — that's what it said in the book. Portia. Pig. We won't be calling our baby that. Pig. Hog.'

'It's not your baby.' Portia had to think fast. 'It's only half your sister. It's not your dad's sperm. It's different sperm. I know all about this. It's only coming out of the same mother. The sperm came out of a different father —' But Ellie had hung up.

In the kitchen Portia's mother was banging tins onto shelves.

'Can I have a rat like Ellie?' Portia got out the milk to make a Milo.

'No.'

'Why not?'

'Because we've got a dog.'
'So?'
'He'd kill the rat.'
'Why?'
'It's in his genes. It's his instinct.'
'What's instinct?'
'What you're born knowing.'
'What's my instinct?'
'Sometimes I wonder, Portia.'
'Ellie's got a dog and a rat. She's got a new rat. It's her second rat. She had a rat that died. It's not fair.'
'The rat lives with her mother, the dog lives with her father.'
'If you and Dad split up can I have a rat? Are you and Dad going to split up?'
'Not this week.'
'Why did you call me hog?'
'What? I didn't. Don't be silly. And don't make a mess.'

But the Milo tin had already popped open, leaving a little heap of brown crystals on the bench.

At her place, Hannah lay on the rug in front of *The Simpsons*. The heater was on and she felt sleepy. When her mother came to call her for tea, her pencil had fallen from her hand, her eyelids were flickering and there was a faint scent of lilac. Hannah's mother slipped out the sheet of paper that lay under one crooked elbow. *Do You Like Portia?* it was headed, with a scale of 1 to 5, and a list of girls' names.

In the morning Hannah couldn't find the survey form and there wasn't time to rule up another one. As she went in the school gate she wondered if Portia would ever be so careless. At breakfast she'd told her mother and father about Portia's survey and her mother had said that when Portia grew up she'd be a politician. She said this in a scathing voice. And then Dad said Portia was probably born a social engineer, whatever that was.

It took Hannah until lunchtime to get hold of Portia's survey and tear it into tiny pieces. When the bell came for the end of eating, she'd followed Sia, Nicole, Ellie and Portia down to the back field. She'd had to time it carefully, keeping close to the bushes before darting out into the open ground and lunging with one stiff arm into the clustered bodies gathered around the paper. She felt it crumple and tear under her hand; she came away with some of it; she was running across the field, her feet drumming now on the asphalt of the tapuwae court, her hands rending the half-page to tiny pieces. She even bit off some of it and spat it out as she ran.

When Portia told Ms Ash that Hannah had torn up her maths project, Ms Ash was busy reasoning with one of the naughty boys and took no notice. After that, all Portia could do was make sure Sia, Nicole and Ellie cut Hannah out for the rest of the afternoon. On the way home she walked ahead of her all the way, the whole two blocks. The only thing she said to her, which was when they were on the crossing, was, 'You keep behind me.'

Hannah watched Portia's blonde head bobbing ahead of her down the plane tree-dappled street and didn't mind at all that she couldn't see her face. It was better that she couldn't, because otherwise Portia would be able to see hers, too, and she might ask her why she was smiling. And then Hannah might tell her by accident that she'd spent the rest of lunchtime drawing up a chart headed *Be Kind Contract*, leaving gaps for five names. She was sure it would be something Ms Ash would approve of.

She'd ring Nicole first, she decided, as she went up her right-of-way. Then Sia, and thirdly Ellie. Last of all she'd ring Portia, and Portia would want to come round and see for herself, and because the contract was Hannah's idea, Hannah would be boss. When Portia saw all the other names she'd have to sign up too. Yes, it was shaping up to be a better afternoon than the one she'd had yesterday. Around the back and past the grapefruit tree she went, through the back door and down the hall to the phone.

Taken in the Rain

    The Marine Mammals Keeper.
    The Ungulates Keeper.
    The Reptile Keeper.
    The Carnivores Keeper.

They knew about one another now. So what?

The Marine Mammals Keeper. Canadian. Almost good-looking. Blond and blue-eyed. Perhaps he was the best of them all. At least he talked about permanency, even if it was on the day he left. She'd rung her friend to tell her about him.

    'He asked me to marry him,' she said.
    'Really?' said her friend.
    'Well, he asked if I'd like to go to Newfoundland with him.'

'That's not the same thing,' said her friend, who was married with a baby.

The Ungulates Keeper. Australian. Definitely the worst. He'd never smelt clean, even after a shower. Perhaps it was because the animals he worked with were so huge. A tonne of manure a day, he'd said.

The Reptile Keeper. Pommy, like her. Extremely fat. She supposed he occupied a middle ground. At first he'd made her feel safe and desirable. She remembered he'd been surprised by her, the night after the pub when she'd . . . never mind. Best to forget it. Perhaps he was a mistake. At least the other three were educative. She'd learned a lot about animals. Educative. Yes. That's what they were.

The Ungulates Keeper came with the first ring. His long skinny dick gave one uncomfortable jab just as she reached for the phone. It was the zoo.

'Come quickly,' they said.

'How did they know where to find you?' she asked as they dressed. It wouldn't be too good if the staff had found out already. Especially the Marine Mammals Keeper. He was dishy, but could be moral enough not to step on the Ungulates Keeper's turf.

'I left your phone number with my flatmate,' he said, his hair falling forward in greasy lanks while he pulled on his foul socks.

She caught the ferry to work in the mornings. No matter what the night before had been like, she always arrived at the zoo in a calm mood. Even if the ride had been rough.

The Marine Mammals Keeper showed her a picture of himself riding a whale. 'Killer whales,' he said, 'are gentle.' It was a black and white photograph and very grainy. Taken in the rain, he'd said. But she could pick him out, his big nose above the massive head, gasping for air. Sometimes on the ferry a strange image floated into her mind — the Marine Mammals Keeper deep below the boat, clinging to a huge fish, his pale eyes open and smarting with the salt.

Small men, she thought, sometimes took advantage of their size. They went to sleep on top of you. The Ungulates Keeper did this the second night and she threw him off with the first snore. He landed on his back, his thin arms flung out.

'Do you like going to the beach?' asked the Marine Mammals Keeper.

'Yes,' she said, bending her head over the computer keyboard. She was useless and she imagined that sooner or later they'd find her out. Her references were false. She spent more time reading the 'Help' pop-ups than she did typing.

'I'll pick you up on Saturday, then,' he said, handing her a piece of paper to write her address on. 'About ten.'

The other girl in the office was jealous, she could tell. The Marine Mammals Keeper had the kind of body you used to see in *Cleo* magazine, in the days they had the centrefold.

One night with the Reptile Keeper was enough. She woke in the morning to find him up on his elbow, his plump hand under his chin, staring at her.

'You and I,' he said, 'fit. We're the male and female of the same type.'

Perhaps he was thinking to himself: She'd be safe with the cobras. They couldn't get their jaws around her.

'How about some breakfast?' he said.

He sat at the table with his towel around him and she filled him up with bacon and eggs. Her flatmate was impressed by his corpulence, agog over her cornflakes at his hairy belly.

'Must be off,' he said, and at the door, 'Thanks.'

'Where is he off to?' asked her flatmate.

'To pick up his wife from the interstate bus.'

Jemoona's baby lay grey and wrinkled in the straw like a giant used condom. The Ungulates Keeper stood in an attitude of homage, his wet arms glistening and clasped in front of him. Jemoona nudged the baby with her trunk and made a strange noise.

No, it wasn't Jemoona. It was the Ungulates Keeper. He was crying.

'Sorry,' he said later, in the car. 'It always gets to me, you know?'

The street-lights were going off.

'Mind if I don't come in?' he said, outside her place.

As they looked for a place to lay their towels she yawned.

'Late night?' asked the Marine Mammals Keeper.

'Mmm,' she said.

He wore a pair of very brief black togs and spent most of the day in the water.

'Come for a swim?' he said, still damp from his last one.

'I'm not swimming in that crap,' she said. 'Haven't you heard about the pollution?'

'Good enough for the fish,' he said, 'good enough for me.'

And he ran for the waves. She went to sleep and got burnt.

'I worked for a private zoo when I was in the States,' she had told her prospective employer.

'Really? Where?' he asked.

'Lydia Mills, South Carolina,' she'd said.

Actually it was a private hospital. Hospital. Zoo. What's the difference?

The Reptile Keeper filled the door and signalled to her. She went to him.

'I've got a room at the back of the Snake House,' he whispered. 'With a bed in it. When's your lunch break?'

'Sorry. No go,' she said, going back to her desk. Sometimes — not often — it paid to be blunt.

'This'll help,' said the Marine Mammals Keeper, rubbing in coconut oil. He steadied himself on the back of the sofa, leaving a greasy mark.

'God, you're so soft. Not like the seals. They're kind of . . . kind of turgid.'

'Mmm,' she said, wishing he'd stop. It hurt.

'Roll over,' he said.

'I'm not burnt there,' she said, but turned over. She was glad she did.

'Dolphins,' he said later, 'make love all day long.'

After a while it fell into a kind of pattern. The Ungulates Keeper during the week, one or two nights, but the weekends reserved for the Marine Mammals Keeper.

'I work part time in a restaurant in the weekends,' she told the Ungulates Keeper. 'And sleep in whatever time I have left.'

'I need my energy for the big fish during the week,' said the Marine Mammals Keeper. 'But the weekends are for you, my little fish, my donut.'

The Ungulates Keeper got quite good at it after a while.
'You'll have to tell me what to do,' he said. 'I'm not used to it.'
'Don't elephants have clitorises?' she asked.
He shrugged.
'They like it, though,' he said. 'Next time we put the bull in I'll let you watch.'

The Marine Mammals Keeper was no fool. He had a Master's in Zoology.
'I've been offered a job,' he said, 'in the Antarctic on a research programme. I think I'll take it.'

The Carnivores Keeper caught her eye. It was her hair. Thick and red, to the waist.

'When do you leave?' she asked.
'A fortnight,' he said. 'Can't wait.'
'What is it?' she asked, her ice-cream melting into the sand. 'The research?'
'Environmental impact study,' he said. 'The French have built a runway, everybody else is building bases and blasting for minerals. Already thousands of animals have died.'
'I like to think,' she said, 'of the poles as these pure twin places at either end of the earth.'
'No longer,' said the Marine Mammals Keeper. 'They're being fucked over like everywhere else.'
'But I insist on thinking of them like that,' she said. 'They

won't be ruined, will they? Nobody would want to live there. It's too cold.'

The Carnivores Keeper passed her on the way out the gates to the ferry. Her hair flamed and leapt. Inside her eyes, which suddenly engulfed her, there were glittering girders like the Harbour Bridge with the sun behind it. All the Carnivores Keeper did was look at her and she felt as though she had been kissed.

It was time, perhaps, to give the Ungulates Keeper the flick. She was tired of him. He'd told her all his stories and they were as sad as the Antarctic.

'If the African elephant is killed at the same rate for very much longer,' he said, 'it will be extinct in the wild in twenty years.'

'Mmm,' she said, examining her arm, now as white as before. 'But how do you kill something with skin as thick as an elephant's?'

'Shoot it,' he said. 'Or poison the water holes. That way the babies die too, the ones without the ivory.'

She leaned out of bed for her hand cream.

'Is that what they want them for?' she asked. 'The ivory?'

She rubbed cream into her elbows.

'Yeah,' he said. 'Just the ivory.'

'Ivory is beautiful though, isn't it?'

She was remembering in England, in her grandmother's house, the old piano with real ivory keys. And how her grandmother's plump hands slid over the keys without much feeling, but how it was quite nice and tinkly from out in the garden where you could play in a sun that didn't burn.

'Ivory is only beautiful on an elephant,' said the Ungulates Keeper.

'Ivory can be beautiful on its own,' she said. 'Carved into tiny worlds.'

She was remembering Singapore, where she'd seen the carvers at work. The Ungulates Keeper sighed and rolled over heavily. Quite often, at the end of affairs, she let the bloke finish it. She'd done this in Lydia Mills. First the General Surgeon and last the Gynaecologist. It demanded a fair amount of careful engineering, to be somehow infinitesimally more 'herself' than she already was.

'I've seen the Chinese carvers at work,' she persisted. 'With tiny knives and eyepieces.' She held her thumb and forefinger in a circle. 'Inside a piece of ivory this big they could make a paddy-field, with buffalo and workers in conical hats and individual spears of rice.' The Ungulates Keeper was silent, but awake. She squirted some more hand cream into her palm and began rubbing it into her thighs.

'Surely a little piece of ivory like that wouldn't make any difference?' she said.

And the Ungulates Keeper, on cue, got out of bed and left.

The Marine Mammals Keeper loved her arse. Sometimes he rubbed himself between her buttocks until he spouted like a whale. She didn't mind him doing it, although she was irritated by his requests for her to move. Why should she move? There was nothing in it for her. You only moved like that for men you loved. She'd never loved any man, not properly. Men loved her, though, she knew. She was soft and white and, they thought, sort of helpless.

The Marine Mammals Keeper loved her. He took handfuls of her buttocks and kneaded them, willing her to arch her back and wriggle, wriggle, wriggle just a little bit.

'I've never been to the Antarctic,' she said, as he nose-dived into the pillow.

'Ah,' he puffed. 'Is that what you were thinking about?'

He needed an explanation for her lack of interest. She didn't answer.

'Of course you haven't,' he said, rolling off. 'Why should you go to the Antarctic?'

'I've been nearly everywhere else.'

'Have you been to Canada?'

'Yes. When I was little. With my father. He's a nomad, like me.'

'What about your mother?' asked the Marine Mammals Keeper.

'Dead,' she said. 'I lived with my grandmother and went on holidays with my father.'

She counted on her fingers. Five days until he left.

'The first country I went to my own,' she said carefully, 'was Japan. I worked in a factory where they processed minke whales.'

The Marine Mammals Keeper yawned. 'You've got a funny little sense of humour,' he said.

'Then I went to Iceland where I worked in a fish factory. The nets would come in filled with drowned seals and porpoises.'

The Marine Mammals Keeper sprang out of bed.

'You're joking, surely,' he said.

'No, I really went to those places on my own.' She handed him a tissue to wipe her back.

'Have a shower,' he said. 'It's easier.'

'Easier for you,' she said, getting up.

When she came back there was a note on the pillow.

'Suddenly remembered something I had to do,' it said. 'Will take you out on Wednesday — my last night.'

'Look,' she said to the Carnivores Keeper, 'he's limping.'

Inside his tiny cage the lion paced on three paws.

'He had a piece of glass removed,' said the Carnivores Keeper. 'It's still sore.'

'A piece of glass?'

'Someone threw a bottle at him,' said the Carnivores Keeper. 'It hit the back wall.'

The lion, now she looked at him, did have a tragic aspect to the hang of his head.

And the Carnivores Keeper, sensing her empathy, slid her warm arm around her waist.

The Reptile Keeper came into the office with a sick snake in a box. It was not zoo policy to carry sick snakes in boxes.

'I'd carry him around in my pocket if my trousers weren't so tight,' he said. 'He needs to be kept warm.'

'Put him in an incubator, then,' said the Marine Mammals Keeper, who was seated, casually, on her desk.

'It's not the same. He needs personal contact,' said the Reptiles Keeper, then pointedly: 'I know somewhere ideal. Very warm and wet.'

'Where's that?' asked the Marine Mammals Keeper.

'Did you know,' asked the Reptile Keeper of all assembled, 'that my wife has left me?'

'Don't look at me like that,' she said. They were in a crowded pseudo-Spanish restaurant, brightly lit. Looks like that should be reserved for the dark, so that the one being looked at couldn't see the look, she thought. 'It's as if you want to eat me.'

'I want to go to bed with you,' said the Carnivores Keeper, a long strand of red hair floating in her wine.

'All right,' she said.

It was the taste of the sea and warmth of all mammals.
It was the embrace of like to like.
It was the release of something caged to the wild.
'Tonight?' asked the Carnivores Keeper, her hair still wet from the bath.
She shook her head. It was Wednesday.

She met the Marine Mammals Keeper by the seal pool. He was lying on his tummy, stroking their heads.
'Goodbye, my lovelies,' he said.

'Do you mind if we don't?' he asked her. 'I'm exhausted and I've got a long journey tomorrow.'
But he couldn't help himself, his suitcases by the door and a rare yearning for permanence. Out of habit, she addressed him with her buttocks.
'As white,' he said between them, 'as the Poles.'
They woke early.
'I'll be two months in the Antarctic,' he said, 'and after that it's home to Newfoundland. Will you meet me there?'
'I'll think about it,' she said.
After he'd gone, she rang her friend.
'He asked me to marry him,' she said.

The Carnivores Keeper loved her. They hardly slept. It was a new country. And the Carnivores Keeper was so proud. Everybody at the zoo knew. She sat on her desk at lunchtime and fed her tidbits between kisses.
One day the Carnivores Keeper said, 'I'm tired of all this

travelling. I spend half my life on trains. Let's live together.'

'That's not a good idea,' she said. 'I'm leaving soon.' It was necessary to tell her before any plans were made.

'When?' whispered the Carnivores Keeper.

'In a month. My grandmother is ill.'

It seemed necessary to lie.

The Carnivores Keeper sulked. She hid at lunchtime. She turned away at night. She had roaring tantrums. She stopped eating.

On her last night they went to the same restaurant they'd been to before. The Carnivores Keeper's hair was rough and dull, her eyes were puffy and she refused to order.

'Do you love me?' asked the Carnivores Keeper.

'I don't know.'

The Carnivores Keeper's eyes were dirty brown bits of ice. The restaurant was filling up and the jukebox had gone quiet.

She finished the bottle of wine and realised she'd have to make the Carnivores Keeper hate her. From her purse she fished forty cents and handed it to her.

'Go and put a song on,' she said. 'Something for me.'

The Carnivores Keeper squeezed her fingers as she took the money, but she wouldn't meet her eyes.

There was a brick wall, the wrought iron bars, the long mane. There was a bottle.

And then she was standing, taking it by the neck and hurling it at a spot just above the Carnivores Keeper's head. Pieces of green glass glittered in the Carnivores Keeper's hands and face and dregs of red wine slipped from the wall to her prostrate body.

Thousands of feet above the earth she thought of them all below her, going about their daily business, thinking of her, missing her. She decided it was the community aspect of life in hospitals and zoos that she liked. It was the effort everybody made for the common good that made them such friendly places. However, to find work in either type of institution in England would be like reliving history. She had to branch out into something else.

A flight attendant handed her a copy of *Time* with a photograph of Tony Blair on the front cover. Of course. Politics. Why hadn't it occurred to her before? She imagined that politicians with their sedentary and mostly interior lifestyles would be softer and paler than their zoo-keeper counterparts. Possibly, despite the relative distance from animal manure, they would be sourer smelling. People who had stressful jobs often stank, she'd noticed. Bad smells were something she could live with, though. Hospitals and zoos abounded with them. Politicians were generally older than zoo-keepers, though, and perhaps she would benefit, therefore, by having more highly skilled lovers.

She smiled, a tremor of anticipation running through her body. As soon as she disembarked she would take the train to visit an old friend of her grandmother's. He was sure to wield some influence, after his thirty years in the House of Lords. All she needed was a little job, perhaps as a receptionist in the foyer. Somewhere she would be noticed by the men and women who held the steering wheel and gear-stick of the nation.

Parliament! What havoc she would wreak! What a challenge, somehow to be infinitesimally more herself, and this time with global consequences.

Clumsy Machine

Sometimes he wondered what the medical profession was coming to. Things had certainly changed since he was a youngster, seething with an anguished mixture of self-doubt and self-righteousness, straight out of medical school. Now, disgust rose in him like bile. That young chap over there, with the great mound of hair and tie-dyed shirt — how could he instil confidence in patients dressed like that? He was probably one of those turncoat GPs who favoured small bottles of pretend medicine and home-births.

Since the early sixties, twenty years ago, when he'd taken up his Remuera rooms, Mr Kitchener had favoured three-piece suits, hair-cream and bifocals. A stern-faced, white-starched receptionist, polished mahogany furniture and the odd false bone lying about seemed to instil in Kitchener's patients the kind of respect a doctor needed to survive. A respect verging on awe — awe that in some of the more nervous types spilled over into terror. The most nervous types were usually young mothers visiting him for the first time with babies sporting some kind of deformity. Their clear eyes would widen and pop as he outlined the surgery required, using the longest possible medical words. He was quite aware that most of the mothers had no idea what he was talking about, that he had lost them in the first few minutes. He'd perfected the technique of not letting them know he knew of their confusion, by turning his face to the light and allowing it to glare on his bifocals. That way his eyes, which might give something of this away, were concealed. He could get on with it. By the time he'd finished the women would be so baffled he could just shunt them out the door with no questions asked. Twenty minutes maximum per patient. It was an economical rule in terms of both financial return and his own energy. By its nature, its uniquely impersonal intimacy, surgery made for professional distance.

The manager of the CHE rose to speak. He was, in Kitchener's opinion, a complete fool. The recent cuts to orthopaedics had been major, sweeping and imprecise. The young doctor in his tie-dyed shirt had leaned back in his chair and closed his eyes. Bored or despairing? thought Kitchener. Possibly both. He lowered his glasses and glared over the top.

Wake up, young twerp! he thought. The young doctor opened his eyes to meet Kitchener's. He blushed and worked his buttocks backwards on the squeaky vinyl chair. By his pasty complexion Kitchener judged him to be a vegetarian. And a GP. He'd never met a surgeon yet, orthopaedic or otherwise, who didn't enjoy meat.

The chairman was introducing somebody, a hard-faced woman on his left. She stood and began to speak. American.

Another horrendous 'overseas expert' telling us how to decimate our health system, thought Kitchener. He closed his eyes.

After a moment the warmth of the theaterette and the rush of humidity from the faulty air-conditioning turned to something else. Ah. Fiji. That lovely holiday with his second wife in 1973. Lying on the beach, or by the pool, sipping cool alcohol and retiring to their bure, a bit pissed, for an afternoon of slippery sex. Rhonda had been keen on sex then. She'd liked the reassuring bulk of him, and his clean scrubbed hands. She'd squeaked and wriggled very convincingly. Later in life, of course, she'd told him she'd never enjoyed it, not properly. She told him she'd just given up hoping for an orgasm. She didn't use that word, though — she called it a climax. She'd told him she probably could have had one, if he'd taken the trouble. People were so clinical these days. It occurred to him that as the public became more technically articulate, the medical profession became less so. It was a paradox . . .

Rhonda in those days, though — what eyes . . . what tits . . . what . . . what . . . What? That squeaking again. Rhonda? Kitchener opened his eyes.

It was that young GP, wriggling in his chair, the vinyl against his jeans. He was looking right at him. Kitchener glowered back and the GP lowered his eyes.

'It's my belief,' the American was saying, 'that the medical profession of this country would benefit greatly from a more competitive system. What price excellence? What price endeavour and enterprise? What price —'

Kitchener burped discreetly, behind his hand. The scallops mornay of his lunch — not very discreetly — returned. A dull ping of pain emanated from his prostate. The body. What a clumsy machine. He wondered, suddenly, at the sense of spending a life devoted to rearranging the scaffolding in others and ignoring his own health. As a young man he had been described, by his mother in particular, as strapping. He'd come close to selection for the All Blacks; he'd run like a hound and swum like an otter. In his forties he'd given up smoking and the evening Scotch. Until recently he'd been described, by his wife in particular, as well preserved. No longer. He rubbed a hand over his sparse hair.

He would be well remembered, though. He'd made his mark — thousands of them on thousands of people. There was a sense of gratitude in the community at large, and he was a legend among the nursing profession. He couldn't put an estimate on the number of theatre nurses he'd reduced to tears, or remember a quarter of the jokes he'd made at the expense of the anaesthetised, faulty bodies beneath his scalpel. Kitchener specialised in the hips and pelvis. Surgery on that part of the body allowed for exposed genitals, and genitals were good for laughs.

'A peg for the nose!' he'd bark, and as the theatre sister scuttled: 'No! Not hers. Mine!' Kitchener sniggered. He remembered with pride the time he'd made it compulsory for all theatre nurses to wear panties under their pantihose. To reduce pituite fallout, he'd said. He sniggered again and opened his eyes to silence. The American was staring at him. He raised an amiable hand, smiled, and she continued, glancing over at him now and again. He forced his face to give out an attentive expression to the room at large. A clock. Was there one?

Ah. Above the American's head, but he couldn't quite place the small hand. Half past something. Must be two. Only half an hour since the meeting began.

God help me, thought Kitchener. This could go on forever.

The manager rose and thanked the expert. Everyone clapped

politely, but most of the faces looked closed. A year ago, two years ago, every professional was worried about cuts to their department. Now the concerns were far more personal — everyone was expendable. Kitchener squinted to either side. A lot of the old faces were gone, either by attrition or early redundancy.

A great pity, thought Kitchener. Many of them were the best the country had to offer. In his opinion there was nobody to replace them, though of course the board found replacements. His own, for instance. Vittachi.

One of Kitchener's five daughters from his first marriage had kept a black rabbit when she was a little girl. He was called Nigger, which was acceptable in the fifties. It was Nigger who came to mind now as his eyes rested on Vittachi, three rows ahead, on the aisle. The same bulging, timid eyes, the glossy black hair, small, mobile nose. Vittachi had obviously rushed straight here from the wards. He still wore his white coat and name badge and was paying attention to the manager, resting his elbows on his knees. Vittachi was gentle, so the story went, not like your usual orthopod. He took his time to explain things to patients and was respectful to the nursing staff. There was another story, unsubstantiated, that he used acupuncture for pain relief. Acupuncture for bone pain! May as well treat cardiac arrest with a cup of tea.

Now a grey-haired woman was speaking. It was that midwife person whose name escaped him for a moment. She'd caused a lot of trouble in the past, at the maternity hospital. Some of the best obstetricians had gone private, solely because of her. In Kitchener's opinion she should have been shut up years ago. It was barbaric, what she wanted: women labouring at home with no pain relief, with nothing to save them or the infant if there were complications. It struck him that she and he were of an age, possibly the most senior attendees of the meeting. The midwife spoke on, uninterrupted, which never would have happened when she first came on the scene. There wasn't so much opposition to prehistoric and dangerous methods any more. They were perceived as 'natural' these days, and therefore safe.

Kitchener sighed heavily and wondered what Rhonda was doing at home. It was a longing kind of wonder — a desire to be there with her, watching her. He pictured himself in a casual shirt, on the terrace with its view over the pool to Rangitoto, reading the paper, reaching out to tap Rhonda on the backside as she passed with a tray of coffee and cake. And Rhonda turning to look at him, with a wondering smile. Perhaps he'd pull her onto his knee and together they'd sit and watch the garden, the heads of the chrysanthemums bobbing in the breeze. Maybe he could coax her upstairs. How long had it been now? A year, two years, more? Rhonda was only forty-two, twenty years his junior, and she'd never had children herself. Her body was that of a woman in her mid-thirties, but she'd lost interest in sex.

At first, if he'd asked, she'd give him a reason.

'You're never home' was one of them. 'You should have let me have a baby' was another, then 'I'm beginning the change.'

On the rare occasions he was in bed before her, hope would well in his breast. He'd watch her brush her hair, apply face cream, put on her nightie and he'd think — tonight, maybe tonight. But inevitably Rhonda would get into bed, often with an irritating little-girl smile, turn on her lamp and open her book. Once, aeons ago now, he'd taken the book away. She'd clamped her hands to her face and with a tiny, sad voice begged to be left alone. What did she expect him to do? he wondered. Give up on her? Give up on sex? Did she want him to consider himself old, past all that? He wasn't. He most certainly wasn't. And he was home now, wasn't he? He was home all the time.

The midwife was still talking. She was getting emotional.

'If labouring women are treated as ill patients they will think of themselves as ill. The obvious solution is to regard a labouring woman as an individual experiencing great power and strength. Money previously assigned to upgrading delivery suites should be redirected into pre-natal education. Easy births don't just happen on the day, they happen because the woman has been preparing for the birth for many months . . .'

Kitchener brought his hand to his mouth and yawned.

Why doesn't the manager use that greasy manner he was born with to politely shut her up? he wondered. She certainly wasn't speaking for all women. Jean, his first wife, for instance — she'd cried out for painkillers with the first contractions. By the time each of the five children was born, she was out cold.

The midwife returned to her seat amid enthusiastic applause from a group of women somewhere to Kitchener's left. A beeper sounded, high and piercing above the clapping, and Vittachi leapt to his feat. Kitchener watched him as he passed at a fast clip, his glossy head pushed forward ahead of his polished shoes. The older man envied the younger one's escape.

The manager was thanking the midwife and calling on the American to comment. The little blonde had a supercilious expression on her face. As she took her position centre stage she maintained eye contact with the midwife. She would address all her remarks to her: it stood to become a personalised slanging match.

Kitchener wished he had a bleeper too. This meeting was mainly for professionals who were working in women's health — gynaecologist obstetricians, midwives, pre- and post-natal physiotherapists, social workers. Kitchener had only attended because he wanted to see what Vittachi would be up against. Vittachi! Kitchener had taught him everything he knew. After the boy had arrived from Malaysia and re-sat his medical examinations, he'd assisted Kitchener with hip replacements and pelvic surgery, standing across the table. Very often he'd made some extraordinary suggestions and once or twice Kitchener had allowed him to carry them out.

The midwife called out from the floor: 'Yes! But your situation in the United States is entirely different to our —'

'Order!' said the manager.

There was another bleeper and Kitchener had a brainwave. He stood, patting his suit pocket as though it held the offending instrument. Behind him a chair scraped back as the genuinely electronically summoned professional scrambled up, a female house surgeon. Kitchener smiled apologetically at the manager and followed the young woman out.

In the foyer he felt vaguely foolish. Why had he bothered with that charade? He could just as easily have stood and left, with no questions asked. He strode on, purposefully, out into the day. The sun blazed but there was a cold wind, which picked up the dust from the demolition site beyond the carpark and whipped it into his eyes. It was the old nurses' home they were knocking down, a handsome building of pale brick that dated from the Great War, laced with fire escapes. Now it was rubble, mounds of broken stone, with the fire escapes protruding here and there, bent like skinny, entreating arms.

He would go home, he decided, setting off towards his car, which waited in the doctors' carpark behind the administration building. But at the main entrance he paused. Something was drawing him inside, past the admitting desk to the lifts. He pressed the buttons that would take him to the fourth floor, to the ward he used to share with one or two other orthopaedic surgeons, but was now Vittachi's domain.

Kitchener coasted down the polished corridors. There were blue stickers beside at least two-thirds of the patients' names outside the rooms. Blue stickers used to denote that the patient was Kitchener's. Now it meant Vittachi. There was Vittachi himself, bending over a bed that contained a young man. An accident victim, perhaps — his name tag was festooned with stickers: red, yellow, green and blue. Just about every surgeon in the place must have had a go at him. Vittachi was pressing and prodding, speaking too softly for Kitchener, who stood concealed outside the door, to hear.

'Excuse me, sir, can I help you?' It was a nurse, nineteen or twenty, fresh and keen. She had no idea, obviously, of who he was. Kitchener gave her one of his most withering looks and continued on down the corridor. He sensed rather than saw the young nurse stop another nurse, and point after him.

'But that's Mr Kitchener!' the voice came down to him: older, cigarette-roughened. 'Mr Kitchener!'

He turned reluctantly as Nurse Sims hurried up. 'Mr Kitchener! What a surprise! What brings you here?'

'Oh, I, um . . .' He told himself that under no circumstances must he appear hesitant or unsure.

'It must be nearly a year,' Nurse Sims went on. 'Is it? How are you finding retirement? It must be . . .' She was searching for a word. Kitchener observed her. Nurse Sims had never been one of his favourite nurses by any means — she was gushy, talked too much. Though she had always followed his instructions to the letter, unlike some of the more opinionated ones.

'It must be different for you, after such a busy life,' she finished.

Kitchener realised he was scowling at her. He made an attempt — not very successful — to rearrange his face to a more impassive state.

'Well,' he said, 'nice to see you, Nurse Sims. I must be getting on.'

'No, I'm not —' began Nurse Sims, uncertain. 'I'm not Nurse Sims. I'm Roberts. Remember?'

Kitchener didn't. He shook his head.

'Nurse Sims retired a year ago, and I'll retire myself in two. That is, if I don't take early retirement.' Nurse Roberts gave him a wide smile. Of course, now he remembered — Sims and Roberts: he was always getting them muddled up. They both wore glasses thick as bottle bottoms, they both had curly grey hair, they both smelled of cigarette smoke, they both had large, starched bosoms and broad sterns, they both held surgeons in high esteem. Perhaps he should have been kinder to them. One of them — he couldn't remember which — had had a terrible tragedy in her life, a car accident that took out her entire family. Perhaps it was Roberts — there was something defeated about her. He made an effort now.

'Yes,' he said, 'there are not many senior nurses left, not many of your age.'

Roberts was smiling at him, as if she wanted him to go on. He couldn't think of anything more to say.

'Well —' he said again, turning on his heel.

'We have to make room for the young though, don't we, Mr Kitchener?' said the nurse suddenly. She'd laid a hand on his arm! 'It took me such a long time to get used to it. All the changes, you know — not getting the patients ready for Doctors' Rounds, with hair brushed and clean faces; not having proper visiting hours; all the machines. Sometimes I still miss the old ways, but change is usually for the best. Now, that Mr Vittachi — he's a gifted man, isn't he?'

Kitchener met her eyes through the thick glass of her spectacles and felt a sudden rush of anger. They always said 'gifted' when what they meant was 'nice'. Vittachi didn't ruffle feathers or step on toes, that's what it was. He wasn't gifted, he was proficient. Kitchener looked away from her just as Vittachi himself emerged from the accident victim's room, his hands in his pockets, head down. He looked worried. He looked up and saw the broad back of Nurse Roberts and came towards them. Kitchener took a little step to the side, as if he would vanish into one of the side rooms, but Vittachi had seen him.

'Mr Kitchener!' he said, offering his hand. 'What a surprise.'

Kitchener wondered if the man had washed his hands after his prodding and poking. He'd noticed a degree of carelessness among the younger doctors when it came to personal hygiene. Who knew what his hand had grazed against in the patient's pyjamas? Fecal matter?

The nurses were rushed off their feet. Kitchener hadn't spotted any other than Roberts and the young one since he'd been standing there. He could hear their voices though, and the squeaking of their busy feet on the polished floors in the rooms on either side of the corridor. The voices that responded were uniformly youthful — accident victims, pub brawlers. Where were all the hip replacements, the elective surgery? The babies in their frog plasters, the querulous old ladies striving to be brave?

He realised with a start that Vittachi had lowered his hand, that a few moments must have passed while he gazed at him, that he'd no doubt offended the younger doctor.

'Are you visiting a friend?' asked Vittachi.

'No, no.' Kitchener felt a rising panic. Two nurses, pushing a bed and attendant drip stands, came out of the room at their left. Roberts and Vittachi stepped back and Kitchener was separated from them. He took his opportunity, lifted a farewelling hand and turned on his heel, marching off down the corridor to the swing doors at the other end, as he had done so many times before, before his retirement. On this occasion only the ghost of white coat-tails flew behind him and the bevy of earnest house surgeons, fleet in his wake, was spectral. He pushed through the double doors and made his exit.

On this side of the ward there were no lifts, save the service one. Kitchener took the stairs, his heart pounding less with exertion than shame. What had possessed him to come to the hospital in the first place? He pulled his car keys from his pocket and held them, hot, in his hand. It occurred to him on the landing of the third floor that perhaps he should go back and put things to rights — talk normally, say he just wanted to see the ward again. There was a danger of incurring sympathy, though — more than he'd already received from Roberts. The warm keys propelled him on.

Minutes later his foot rested lightly on the accelerator of his shiny red two-seater as he whizzed past the Domain duck ponds. It was warm in the car. The brilliant sun outside lit up the marble of the statue to his left and to his right, above the waving swords of the red canna lilies, the roof of the bandstand glittered. Behind the bandstand, beyond the gleaming cars parked before the cannons, high on its ridge, sat the museum. Like the hospital, it reigned over the city, holding towers of commerce and dwellings of the wealthy in its gaze. Kitchener used to like the way he could look up from certain streets, or from the deck of friends' yachts on the harbour, and see the hospital, the setting of so much of his working life. Now he felt the weight of it behind him, a behemoth hand of stone pushing him away home, home to Rhonda.

It was the middle daughter, the one who'd had Nigger, who was to come to dinner. Rhonda had put their differences aside in favour of an anguished alliance. This had had to do with Kitchener, whom they both openly believed to be difficult but worth the effort, and biological clocks. It appeared that Susan was unable to have children the normal way. She was thirty-two, and she and Alistair had been through the in-vitro fertilisation programme four times with no success. Whereas Susan previously had wanted to discuss only her mother's despair at her husband's betrayal and his second marriage, she now engaged Rhonda in private, esoteric discussions on the female urge to reproduce.

When he had heard they were coming Kitchener had endeavoured to persuade Rhonda to cancel.

'Don't be ridiculous,' she'd said, not looking at him, 'Susan and Alistair are very busy, you know that. We mightn't get another chance for weeks.'

'Invite one of the other girls another night, then,' he'd said. 'They'll come.'

'With all their frightful kids,' Rhonda responded. 'I've told you before: I'm not going to play Grandma when you've never given me a chance to play Mother.'

Kitchener went out for a dip in the pool where, briefly, he considered submersion of several minutes, long enough to end it all. In the end he forced himself out and lay on the warm tiles staring up at the blue Remuera sky, flecked with gold. Two clouds: one approaching from the east, pure white but for blue-grey fluid borders; and the other gleaming orange, lit by the sunset. The second was the larger, hanging in the apex of the heavens, burning with light and streaming towards the west. The odd thing was that both clouds were shaped like hands: the white one lumpy, thick-fingered; the gold one lithe, slender. He counted its five fingers, admired its narrow surgeon's wrist, then realised it was dissolving, losing its shape. The white cloud earnestly prodded and buffeted its golden counterpart and they began to merge.

'Didn't you hear me calling you?' Rhonda had come out of the house, across the terrace and down the steps.

'What's the matter?' she said. 'Are you ill? Clem?'

'Not particularly,' he said.

'What?' Rhonda tapped her foot behind his prone head. 'Speak clearly.'

'No.'

'They'll be here in half an hour. Maybe you could choose some wine.'

After a moment he heard her turn, heard the shift of fabric on fabric as her tight skirt rustled on her underwear, her step. She stopped.

'Have you been drinking?' she asked.

'What a preposterous question.' Kitchener closed his eyes and wished she'd go away.

She didn't straight away. He could hear her breathing, as if she was thinking of something else to say. Fortunately she failed in the quest, sighed heavily and turned back to the kitchen. Kitchener waited until he heard her distant heels on the hard, polished floors of the house, beyond the astro-turf of the terrace, before he hauled himself up. One of his legs had gone numb from lying too long on the tiles. He gave it a hearty slap, which his dull synapses hardly registered, before going to collect his clothes from the pagoda.

Susan had too much perfume on. Though they were on the terrace it stung his nostrils, offended his keen sense of smell. He may never have had narrow wrists — not as narrow as Vittachi's, at least not since he was ten years old — but by Christ he could smell the threat of post-operative infection through a plaster cast before it even took hold. Many times he'd smelt heat and pressure, seconds before a patient haemorrhaged. He could tell the difference between the blood of the anaesthetised old and that of the anaesthetised young; he could smell fear and satisfaction. Susan felt his eyes on her and lifted her glass.

'Dad. What have you been up to?'

'Not much,' he said.

'Pardon?'

Had he spoken too quietly? Susan gave him a strange, querying look and answered her husband. Alistair was saying, 'You should go and get Rhonda out of the kitchen. Tell her to come and have a drink. We haven't even said hello yet.'

Susan stood. 'Yeah. Dinner can wait. We're all grown-ups here tonight! If the ankle-biters were here we'd have to rush.' She flashed a look of cold, wounded betrayal at her husband and departed. A wave of scent broke over Kitchener's head. He took a sip of wine to quell rising nausea.

'Um . . . Clem . . . I hope you don't think I'm out of order, but . . .'

Kitchener examined his son-in-law curiously. He was leaning forward, legs apart, twiddling the stem of his wine glass, thumb and forefinger rolling it back and forth. He was embarrassed — was he blushing? Having not really looked at Alistair since he arrived, Kitchener wasn't sure. Perhaps the man was windburnt. What on earth was he going to say? The atmosphere was leaden, as it had been when two other sons-in-law had told Kitchener they were leaving his daughters. At least this time there were no children and Susan had a well-paid job. The schnauzer would be a problem, though. They both doted on it.

Alistair cleared his throat. 'I . . . um . . .' he continued, '. . . think you've had enough of that.' He inclined his head towards Kitchener's glass.

Kitchener was baffled. Enough of what? He took a sip and thought on it. Enough of sitting in this particular chair, on this particular terrace, in this house, this suburb, this city, this life? True enough. Tonight, that was true enough.

Alistair was staring at him. Kitchener met his eyes and smiled. The women's voices were coming closer.

'You know, I've never seen you . . .' Alistair spoke in a rush, pausing in peculiar places, 'like this something. Must've happened to make you. Do it you could have rung and put. Us off can I get you a glass of water?'

'Alistair!' Rhonda came through, smelling of garlic and roses. Behind her, Susan brought a second wave of opposing scent. Alistair stood and kissed Rhonda on the cheek.

'Let's go through,' said Rhonda, gesturing towards the dining room. 'It's all ready.'

'Have another drink, Dad,' said Susan sarcastically. 'Alistair will pour you one.'

Kitchener caught her withering glance broadside and was wounded by it. It shot into the corner of his eye with a sudden pain. What the devil was going on?

'No, no — I insist! The dinner will spoil.' Rhonda was using her gay voice, the one she usually reserved for the telephone. 'Right now!'

'Yes, Mum,' joked Alistair.

The three of them stood looking down at Kitchener, who sat

cradling his wine glass against his chest. He felt oddly paralysed. Three shadows fell across him. Rhonda's one extended an arm.

'Clem. Will you join us?'

With a lurch, Kitchener propelled himself up out of his rattan chair. His feet were numb, he failed them, he fell over, flat on his face, knocking over the flimsy table with its two bottles of wine: one red, one white. The two liquids coursed around him, merging, red and white to pink. He felt his shirt soak it up to his skin and knew, without a shadow of a doubt, that he'd had a stroke.

At least it was a different ward, though he kept his eye out for Vittachi.

'Medical insurance?' he'd said to Rhonda five years ago. 'Who needs it? You get just as good care in the public system as you do in the private. You're panicking, believing the media.'

And here he was being assessed by bug-eyed, exhausted house surgeons six months out of medical school.

He gave up trying to talk to Rhonda on her daily visits. She talked to him, though, of how she'd arranged for a live-in nurse to look after him when he came home. She obviously had no knowledge of the many cases of stroke where the sufferer had recovered. He would recover. And there wouldn't be a nurse. If he couldn't make his feelings clear verbally, he'd spit on her as soon as he met her. Here came one now, to take his temperature. She shoved the thing in his ear, some electronic contrivance that looked like a gun. At least it spared him the embarrassment the conventional type would afford him — it wouldn't fall out of his slack mouth. Which was full of saliva. Kitchener decided against spitting on this nurse. She would no doubt take it personally.

'I've got one coming tomorrow,' Rhonda was saying, 'for an

interview. Alistair came round and helped me move furniture. We've put you in the dining room downstairs. It looks very nice, a sort of bedsitting room.'

Rhonda prattled on about new drapes and rugs, and the Stanley Palmer she'd hung in there for him to look at. Kitchener tweaked up the mobile side of his face to show he was pleased. Poor Rhonda. The sun slanting across his bed was soporific, enervating.

When he woke Rhonda was gone, and a nurse was rousing him for the evening meal. Purée, thickened with something from a large tin marked Karitane. With one hand she would spoon it in, with the other gently massage his throat to assist swallowing.

Kitchener wasn't hungry. He turned his face away, tried to clench his useless jaws. The nurse got a spoonful in, which fell out again. It had been placed too far forward in his mouth. He took a sneaky look at the nurse, who was placidly reloading the spoon. A shadow moved behind her and a familiar voice said, 'Excuse me, Nurse. I'll do that if you like.'

'Oh . . .' The nurse was uncertain. 'Are you sure? Doctor . . .'

The shadow's hand tapped something plastic on its chest, a name badge.

'Vittachi.'

'Right. All right, then. You know how . . . ?'

Vittachi nodded.

Slowly Kitchener turned his head to look at his supplanter. The nurse stood, handed over the bowl and left to feed someone else. Vittachi put the bowl down on the bedside cabinet.

'You don't want it, do you?' he said, sitting on the bed.

Kitchener couldn't reply. He looked steadily into Vittachi's eyes, which were warm, brown, clever. He could see, suddenly, why the man was so liked. There was a compassionate intelligence about him, something unshockable.

Vittachi waited until the older man looked away, then he said, 'You know, Mr Kitchener, if things were different I'd ask your opinion on something. A case I have. Spondylolisthetic pelvis in an elderly woman. Associated arthritis and osteoporosis. I don't know whether to help her or not. She's seventy-nine.'

Leave her alone, you chump, thought Kitchener.

Vittachi was looking at him earnestly. 'Can you wink?' he asked.

In reply Kitchener shuttered his left eye and reopened it.

'Good,' said Vittachi. 'One wink says I do, two says I shouldn't.'

Kitchener concentrated and gave him two.

'Hmmm.' Vittachi reached for the bowl. 'Hungry now?' he asked.

The interview with Vittachi had made him feel better, Kitchener realised, as Alistair helped him out of the car and into a wheelchair. It had at least made the rest of his stay in hospital bearable. He'd done some good. He'd saved an old lady a lot of needless pain. Alistair looked again towards the house for the nurse to come, while Rhonda fussed over him with a tartan travelling rug.

'Give her a toot,' she said.

Alistair stood up, flicking a gleaming strand of hair out of his blue eyes. A loud horn shattered the air seconds after he passed out of the perimeters of Kitchener's gaze. Kitchener could hear him breathing, hear him shaking the keys softly in a cupped hand. There was no sound from the house.

'She must be stone deaf,' said the son-in-law.

'Maybe — she's certainly no spring chicken!' said Rhonda, with a giggle.

'Will you be all right? I've got to get back.' Was he looking at his watch?

'Don't worry about us. We'll be fine.'

Oh, that velvet voice. He hadn't heard it for a long time. It seemed Rhonda had well and truly risen to the occasion of his illness. When he died she would rise to the occasion again by sitting rigidly in the church, admired by women of her generation for her old-fashioned tearlessness.

'Okay,' said Alistair. 'Bye, then.'

Behind him Kitchener heard a kiss, lips to cheek. Or was it? Rhonda was scenting Alistair's cheek, taking in a deep breath of air, something she did only when she was kissed on the lips. It was something Kitchener did. She'd discovered the delight of it early in their courtship, and now she did it herself.

'I'll ring you later,' from Alistair.

'Thanks, Alistair,' said Rhonda. She began to push Kitchener up the drive.

Behind them Alistair's Alfa Romeo roared backwards into the street.

'Hel-lo!' yodelled Rhonda, but there was still no response from the house.

'See the terracotta tiles on the ramp?' Rhonda was puffing at its gentle incline, 'Alistair designed it to keep in with the style of the house. The railing is custom made.'

Under the tartan rug Kitchener clenched a fist and released it, clenched it again. It was part of his exercise programme.

'Alistair has been marvellous. I can't tell you,' Rhonda went on, 'just how marvellous he's been. Don't be surprised by Susan. I think she's a tiny bit jealous.'

The door stood ajar. It was a new door, Kitchener noted — wide enough to fit his chair through, with no step.

'Hel — lo!' Rhonda yodelled again. The house was hushed, but Kitchener detected something in the air. Five different brands of perfume, the smell of antiseptic, and something else. Baby shampoo. Rhonda flung open the door to what used to be the dining room.

For a moment the changes in the decor were lost on him: popping up from behind the bed, the chest of drawers, the table, the commode, were myriad cheering faces. There were all the daughters and their children, and sailing towards him came the broad white bust of a nurse. Susan's eyes were swollen with tears; the nurse's eyes were hidden behind glasses as thick as bottle bottoms.

'Hello, Mr Kitchener,' said Sims, coming forward. Or was it Roberts? 'Welcome home!'

The Colour of Flesh

You could have sworn that as you woke, you heard the front door open gently and close, a soft click of the snib and my bare foot on the boards; you woke with the sure knowledge that someone had come into the house — but remembered, in the same instant, that the family had gone out, that you were alone, that it was early Sunday evening and that you had fallen asleep, as you never do, in the middle of the day. Here you were, returned to yourself in an armchair, the late sun boisterous at the window, swirling the dust motes into a column that terminated in a bright disc the size of a dinner plate on the carpet, chaotic with abandoned playing cards, just beside your left foot.

You got up and went to the kitchen, turned on the radio and after a moment thought nothing more of me, believing instead that you had been dreaming of a visitor, and entertaining yourself with the notion that the visitor was female. You wondered, while you chopped and peeled, if it was someone you knew — your mother, your sister, a friend — and you wished for a moment that the dream had continued so that you could have found out . . .

And then you gave your attention to your children, who came in from the park with your husband. They ate, ran riot, were bathed, read to and put to bed — a summer Sunday evening like any other. Early on I got sick of watching you, unacknowledged. In a sulk I leaned into a corner of the dining room, only momentarily encouraged by the fact that you laid the table for one more than your family — *she knows, she knows* — but halfway to the table you realised, and took the empty plate back to the cupboard. That's when I gave up, went down to the bedroom and unpacked my vanity case, put on some perfume and waited. By the time you went to bed, yawning and staggering, leaving the husband cast on the couch in full snore, you had forgotten all about me.

Which is why I had to let you see me. Just for an instant. I heard you come in, sniff the scented air, flick on the light. In the mirror above the dressing table you saw a flash of something flesh-coloured, a soft peach-pink, turning away from the onslaught of the bulb: a narrow, girl's body, a smudged whip of dark hair swinging around it.

I watched your tired, sluggish thoughts progress from the mirror to the wardrobe opposite — was there something hanging over the door, a shirt, a scarf? But you possess nothing peach-coloured, the colour does nothing for you: it took you a moment to remember that. You shook your head like a B-grade Hollywood actor, peeled off your clothes and fell under the duvet.

Far too prosaic and pragmatic a case for me, I thought.

In the morning you got the kids off to school, the husband off to work — who thanked you for the back-rub you'd administered to him when he'd finally come to bed, around one in the morning.

'You dreamed it,' you said, because you hadn't massaged him at all. 'When you came in I was fast asleep' — and as he went out the door he laughed as if you were joking.

Then you went to work yourself, moved paper, solved problems, dealt with this and that and him and her, collected the kids from after-school care, came home. So stultifyingly boring was it that after only half an hour I flitted off, only momentarily returning during the day to see if there was anything I could do to help you, but I'm no good at that sort of thing: commerce or business — whatever it is you do at your desk. I was much better employed here, baking the cake that gave you such a surprise when you came in. It was a Dolly Varden, in three coloured layers, all decorated with pink icing and sugared flowers, set out on the dining-room table. I'd had time to do a good deal more — asparagus rolls, sausage rolls, sweetcorn in bread cases, smoked mussels on crackers — but hadn't because I thought you wouldn't want the children to spoil their dinners. But I thought you'd enjoy the cake.

You did not, and neither did I enjoy your response. Nor did the younger children. You freaked out and it frightened them. You rang your mother, who has a key to the house. You rang your husband, who was stuck in traffic on his way home.

'Where'd you learn to do that thing with your tongue?' he asked, immediately he knew it was you — and you had no idea what he was talking about.

'Look,' you almost shouted, 'there's a cake just suddenly materialised on the dining-room table. And there's the smell of baking, though nothing's changed in the kitchen. And last night there was this perfume in our bedroom and I thought I saw —'

But your husband wasn't listening.

'Fantastic — nearly blew the top of my head off — can't figure out how you did it, what exactly you were —'

'No! Stop! We don't know where it's come from!' you interrupted, shouting at the children, who had fetched a knife and were cutting large slices — 'I've got to go.' Meanwhile the oldest child was holding the cake to his nose, sniffing — 'There's nothing wrong with it' — and biting, chewing, swallowing.

You stopped the other two children from ingesting any of the dangerous cake and watched the older one for adverse affects. There were none. You oversaw homework, piano practice. Your husband came home and was unusually demonstrative. You cleared away, and got ready to go out.

'What movie are you seeing?' asked your husband. 'Will Tania meet you there?'

You gave the prepared answers and we drove away, not far. You climbed a dry, wooden fire escape hung with ivy, and made love with a particular man, for the fifth time, which was no surprise to me. That's why I'm here — because of him.

I waited outside, pleased that I'd dabbed a little of my distracting perfume on your throat and wrists before you'd turned off the ignition. As you'd got out you sniffed at the air a little, less than you had in the bedroom, because your mind was full of anticipation. I fell asleep — or at least suspended the peculiar molecules of my being in the closed atmosphere of your car — until you returned, every cell thrumming, and drove us home.

The next evening you returned home to a beef and red wine casserole bubbling on the stove and all the washing done and folded. Your husband said it was the best thing you'd ever cooked and made another puzzling reference to your anatomy — not your tongue this time but your derrière which, until last night — he whispered in your ear on returning his plate to the kitchen —

he'd never known could be so accommodating.

'What are you talking about?' you asked, but your husband only gave you a licentious wink before he went to his study to put in a couple of hours of paperwork. After the children were in bed you longed to ring your lover. You hadn't mentioned the cake to him. Or the perfume. Now there was the casserole and the laundry. It was all too much.

And you did ring him, after ten o'clock, from the gloom of the garden, sitting on the swing, hoping your husband wouldn't pick up the phone inside the house. You could see him illuminated in the study window at his desk — you could perhaps watch him and make sure he didn't make a sudden lunge to make a call — but it was hard to concentrate on dialling your lover while watching your husband. I managed to effect three wrong numbers, and you did one of your own, but you were determined and finally got through, to discover he was with someone and couldn't talk.

If only you had let me spare you the agony.

That night you woke in the dark to a leaden exhaustion and chilled through to the marrow, as if you hadn't been asleep at all but climbing hand-over-hand the icy south face of a mountain. You opened your eyes to my shadow astride your husband, my ghostly tush in congress with his fleshly rod, the wraith of me thrashing in spectral ecstasy.

'Who are you?' you asked aloud, sitting up.

'I'm the Spirit of Absolution,' I told you, but I don't think you heard me because you were shouting —

'Get away from our bed!' And your husband, groping for the switch, flooded the room with light.

'Wha — wha — what?' went your husband, sleepy dirt in his eyes and saliva strung from top lip to lower in silvery strands.

'There was a woman here,' you started. 'A young woman in our bed . . . she was on top of you, she was —'

'You're working too hard. Or missing some vitamins. Go back to sleep,' he said, and turned off the light again with a heavy sigh.

The third night I made porterhouse steak for your husband, curry of fish for you and roast chicken for the children: everybody's favourites. When you tried to tell your husband that the meals were not prepared by your own hands, you were so alarmed you could hardly shape your words. You stuttered, which is most unlike you, who are usually so emphatic and precise.

'What's wrong with you,' said your husband, without an upward inflection, as if he didn't expect an answer. 'All this false modesty.'

The fourth day I carved a giant ice swan as a centrepiece for the table; the fifth I wove a tapestry, full of concupiscent satyrs and obliging nymphs, to cover the bedroom wall. On the sixth I prepared for your next visit to your lover, but your husband was already suspicious the night of the swan.

'How'd you get time to do that?' he asked, and when he saw the tapestry he said, 'That's tacky — but I quite like it. How much was it? Your tastes have changed . . .' And he looked at you with a little more curiosity than usual.

On the sixth night he wondered only at your bloodshot eyes and what was for dinner. It was as if you'd already got so used to me, in the space of a week, that you took me for granted. I hadn't been near the kitchen, of course. I'd spent the day beside your lover, listening to his phone calls, watching him work. Sells real estate, doesn't he? A real terrier, isn't he? Though in essence he's not a bad man, your lover, even taking into account his string of married women.

You sobbed in the bathroom while your husband went up the road for takeaways and the children watched television. It was inevitable, you told yourself. Pull yourself together; don't ever do it again.

And I don't believe you will.

The tapestry was gone from the wall by the time you came out, and all my misty perfumes were back in the vanity case. I slipped away out the door as your husband came in, flew across town and zipped up a wooden fire escape, dry as tinder, hung with ivy. His flat is disgraceful, his fridge empty, his ashtrays overflowing, his conscience burdened and soiled.

He doesn't know I'm here yet. He ignores me, much as he negated you. But I'm not worried, not yet. I wash his sheets, pick hair out of the plug, never let the Scotch bottle fall below half full, make sure there's milk for his tea. There are no other demands on my time; I'm a free agent.

I can absolve all the guilt in the world. Tonight in the mirror I will let him see me: my young boy's narrow body, newly manifested, and the blue flash of my innocent eyes.

Fable

The house was finished. Any fool could see that it was: you only had to look up from the flats and there it was on the point of the bluff, a finished house in the colonial style, tall and white with a wide verandah and green-gabled roof.

The builder had kept pretty much to himself and now that it was finished — or so people said it was — he was less in evidence than ever. Before that, before he finished the house, he used to come down the loose metal-chip road in his truck to the town and park in the wide, empty carpark outside Mann Brothers Building Supplies. Billy Mann and whichever of his brothers were around, if any, would help him load up the wooden floor joists and joinery, or white plastic weatherboards, or shining aluminium window frames, or sheets of green roofing iron. Once or twice the little truck — which suffered badly from rust, living as it did surrounded on all sides by the sea — was loaded down with bricks for the chimneys and verandah posts. On these occasions it would crawl slowly home along the bluff road, up and down the two low hills that rose like knuckles on the finger of land, its tray low on the springs, gears graunching.

'It's a ka pai house he's building up there, all right,' said the Mann brothers and the hundred or so other people left living in the town. Truth be told, the Mann brothers didn't want the house ever to be finished. It was all that was keeping them in business, which was sad, because the brothers had thought four years ago that they had a bright and prosperous future. That was when the Maori Investment Board gave Tikiruru the grant. During the many hui out on the marae there was talk of a golf course, a five-star hotel, a cinema complex and a games parlour and Billy thought he was doing well by getting in first with the building supplies. But the money was gone — vanished, melted away — and nobody knew where. In Wellington the few MPs who were thick-skinned enough to be oblivious to accusations of racism tried to instigate an enquiry, but even that had vaporized, their initial fury overcome by an amnesiac torpor and apathy, eerie and swift in effect.

Now it was a good day for Billy when a farmer's wife came in for a roll of wallpaper, or the Tikiruru Takeaways needed a tin of paint to spruce up their sign on the main road, or a kuia needed a new washer for a tap. Before the construction on the now-finished house began there were weeks when Billy, his square hands on the wide counter, sold only a packet of nails, and it seemed business had returned to its somnolent state. Billy's wife packed up the kids and some household effects and left for Auckland, for a better life, but Billy wasn't sure he wanted to give up, not just yet. He had a feeling things were going to improve.

One sunny winter morning, as he sat on the back step of

Mann Brothers Building Supplies with his lonely mug of tea, Billy lifted his eyes from the sea. He'd been contemplating locking up and going fishing — there were gulls and gannets working off the bluff — when something near the finished house caught his attention. Rising above the pohutukawas, which wound around the cliff face and fenceline, was another roof. It was smaller than the finished one, but the same colour, pitch and gable. A garage built with the leftovers, thought Billy, to put the orange truck in. He took a sip of his cooling tea and squinted: there on the smaller roof was the builder himself, his shirt off and astride the gable, a brown and rectangular object taking shape before him. A chimney.

You don't put a chimney on a garage, thought Billy, just as a cloud uncovered the sun and set a tiny dormer window flaring. Nor does a garage require a dormer window. Fishing plans forgotten, Billy set off on foot along the beach to where the hill dropped down to a valley, to a spot where you could take a sheep path along the point.

As he walked Billy puffed a little, the old rugby injury in his left knee ached and he longed for the days before his wife left, when he could have driven along the metal road. But she had taken the car. Further on, where the sea chomped and hissed at the rocks ten metres below in a vertical drop, he thought how strange it was that he still didn't know the builder's name. The man had always paid cash, so there were no order forms or invoices to fill out. He never went to the marae or the near-deserted church, or to the pub on Route 1 next to Tikiruru Takeaways. He kept himself a man apart. Billy turned his eyes away from the drop — in the days when there were sheep here, quite often one of their number would fall to the rocks. One wrong step and he could too . . .

There was something old fashioned about the builder, thought Billy as he went along the narrow dirt path, one foot directly in front of the other. Something in his manner reminded him of his own grandfather, now dead. The builder always called him Mr Mann and thanked him for his trouble; he even doffed his hat. His accent, now — it was a kind of non-accent, with all the clarity and lucidity of water. Billy couldn't place it, or even the man's race. He wasn't from around here, he knew for sure, and he probably wasn't Maori — though there was no telling these days.

At the gate, which stood ajar, its lower corner lifted to the grass mound between the wheel ruts, he paused for a breather and turned around to survey the rise of the hill beside him. Something about it gave him a start and it took him a moment or two to work out what it was. The gorse. It was gathered together in a collar around the crest of the hill, in a kind of hedge, contained and low-growing, like a row of ornamental shrubs. All the farms here and around were covered in gorse, great rampant spiky clumps turning whole hillsides yellow in the summer. How had the builder made his gorse behave like that? Billy wondered, turning and passing through the gate. He would make a point of asking him.

It's never a good idea to call out to a man on a roof — you could startle him — so Billy continued in his soft jandal tread along the now-level road to the house. The trees the man had planted — poplars, cypress, gums and oak and others that Billy didn't recognise — had grown faster than you would have expected; some of them looked as though they'd been in the ground twice as long as they had been. You could forget which country you were in up here, thought Billy; you could be anywhere.

The builder wasn't up on the roof at all. He was sitting on the verandah of the finished house, a little table at his elbow, and on it was a tall frosted brown bottle of beer and two glasses. He had his shirt off still and Billy, as he came up the low steps to shake his hand, couldn't help noticing the builder's chest hair: thick, brown and glossy. It was more like the hair off a head, or an animal, he thought. The builder must have felt his eyes on it because he coloured slightly and turned away to pick up his shirt from the other chair. He put it on.

'Nice to have a visitor,' he said, gesturing at the chair for Billy to sit down, which Billy did gratefully.

'Did you see me coming from the roof?' asked Billy, accepting a glass.

'Eh?' The builder looked momentarily startled, as if he might deny he'd been on the roof at all, but he went on, 'Yes — yes. I saw you coming.'

'The other roof, I mean. The little roof.' Billy rubbed at his knee, which pained him.

'Oh yes. The little roof.' The builder took a sip of beer, slow and careful, as if he was worried he'd spill it, or misdirect it down the wrong tube and choke. He made a strange bobbing motion with his head and Billy wondered if he always drank like that. He'd never seen him drink before.

'What is it?' Billy persisted. 'I didn't know you were planning on building another place.'

'It's, um . . . well, I don't know what you'd call it,' the builder said. 'Is there a name for it?'

Billy looked at the smaller building, which stood directly in front of them. It was almost a complete copy of the finished house, even to the verandahs, but on a smaller scale, as if it was a playhouse for a rich man's child.

'A sleep-out?' he asked.

The builder looked startled again and then he laughed, a sudden, breathy laugh mixed with dry, dental clicks.

'That's good!' he said. 'Very good. A sleep-out — yes, that's what it is.'

'It'll block your view,' observed Billy, 'from your downstairs, anyway.'

'Oh,' said the builder neutrally, as if he didn't care much for views.

'Mind if I take a look inside the finished house?' asked Billy, standing up, his glass drained.

'Suit yourself. There's nothing much to see.'

Billy was already at the door, turning the handle, which offered enough resistance to compel him to lean his considerable weight against it. Perhaps it had swollen in the rain, he thought, then recalled that the winter so far had been a dry one. It opened, finally, with the creak of ancient hinges — which, had he paused to think about it, Billy would've found as curious as the collar of gorse to the west of the house.

The room he stepped into was vast, empty and, because of the verandah awnings shading the light, gloomy. At first, while his eyes adjusted, Billy thought the looming grey shape against the far wall was a sofa, until he perceived, with a slight chill down his spine, that it was thick roll of dust, a century's worth at least, rolled into a giant oblong under the smeary window. There was no furniture at all, the walls raw gib and the floor uncovered particle board. The room darkened again and Billy turned to see the shape of the builder, silhouetted against the bright daylight. A strong smell pervaded the room, as if animals had been kept in here, or winter feed.

'This is the sitting room?' he asked.

The builder nodded, the rapid bobbing motion again.

'What's through there?' Billy pointed towards a closed door on his left and the builder's shoulders lifted and dropped in a shrug.

'Another room, I think,' he said. 'It's a long time since I've come in here.'

'But —' Billy started to say that it can't have been that long, that the house had only been finished for a couple of months. But something made him leave the remark unspoken; a threat rose from the man at the door, more powerful than words. *Come away.* It was a command. *Come away before you are hurt.*

The builder stepped aside to let Billy pass.

'It was good to see you,' he said as Billy drew level with him. It was a dismissal.

'Yes,' said Billy uncertainly. He wondered now if he should have drunk the beer — if the brew had been safe, or normal — but now, here he was at the gate, with no recollection of having got that far. It annoyed him — he'd wanted to look in the windows of the sleep-out, to see if that building had the trimmings you'd expect: bunks, a cupboard, maybe a kitchenette.

The beer wasn't poisoned, although as Billy had to admit as he stepped inside Mann Brothers Building Supplies on return from his long walk, he was very tired. He sat down on the armchair he kept behind the counter and fell into a deep sleep, from which, on waking, his visit to the finished house paled and blurred into the memory of dream.

Winter, such as it was this far north, passed quickly and spring arrived with the temperatures of midsummer. Billy's youngest brother Mack arrived with his family and they set up their caravan in the paddock behind Mann Brothers Building Supplies for a holiday by the sea. From time to time, ever since that difficult-to-remember day, Billy had cast a wary eye up to the bluff. From the flats the collar of gorse showed only as a fine black line and the trees had grown so thick and fast around the finished house and its miniature that only a corner of green roof was visible.

On New Year's Eve Billy's brother wanted some action; he was restless and argumentative. After he'd quarrelled with his wife and she'd taken herself off to bed, Mack smoked a joint and drank on, filling Billy's glass as frequently as he filled his own.

'Let's go up there — I want to see what kind of spread he's got,' Mack said, reeling slightly, his arm a dark, wavering pointer in the moonlight. Billy shook his head.

'Might be a party,' said Mack, and he took off along the beach in a slow jog. After a short while Billy followed him, foreboding dulling his blood: Mack could ask questions the builder might not like; he might not leave when he was asked to — or not asked, as the case could be. He might not even make it that far, being drunk and stoned and the sheep path narrow, the cliffs precipitous.

'Mack,' Billy called in a low voice when he reached the dip in the hill, the first knuckle of the point. Only silence answered him, the whirring of crickets, the steady thump and suck of the surf, the cry of a distant night bird. He kept inland from the sheep path by a metre or so, his jandals slipping and sliding on the clean grass.

'Mack!' he called again at the gate, which stood as open as it had before. 'You there?'

The crickets were quiet, the sea muted. Hot breath burned his throat; fear pulsed at his temples, making his eyes ache.

'Bugger you, Mack.'

A dim light glowed in the finished house and as Billy got closer he could see it emanated from the same downstairs room he had gone into on his visit. Crouched outside the window was his brother, intent on whatever he could see inside.

'Mack —' Billy whispered. His brother remained transfixed, holding up a hand to silence him. Billy came close, treading as softly as he could on the creaking verandah timbers. Side by side, they pressed their faces to the glass.

A long, candlelit table ran from one end of the room to the other. Curiously, the room seemed bigger, thought Billy. Usually the introduction of furniture and a crowd of people made a room seem smaller. And there was a crowd — the builder must've invited friends for the summer. How the guests had got there was a puzzle: the brothers had passed no cars parked in the driveway, and now that Billy thought about it, he hadn't seen any cars zipping along the metal-chip road.

At one end of the table sat a woman in a fur coat. How hot she must be, Billy thought sympathetically, rather over-heated himself from the pursuit of his brother. Crowded, buck teeth glimmered in the candlelight within her thin-lipped mouth. To her right sat a tiny man, whose hair stood straight up on his head in spikes. He was intent on the woman beside him, who carried a baby in a front-pack, her chair pushed away from the table to accommodate it. Her husband — Billy supposed he was her husband — sat beside her, a shiny-haired, cool-looking individual with wraparound gold-coloured sunglasses. The chair beside him was empty and the one after that, the third along, was occupied by a man with a long, pointed nose and eyes so small they were scarcely discernible. The man sat slumped, morose, the chairs on his other side continuing vacant. He must have offended the others, Billy thought.

After a gap, the line of guests resumed with a thin, narrow-boned woman dressed in luminous chlorophyll green. She was doing her best to ignore the woman beside her, whose long, twisted locks of hair cascaded over her shoulders and ample body right onto the table. She was the most vivacious of all of them, laughing and tossing her head so that the ends of her hair dangled in various of the guests' water glasses. The next guest wore a Viking hat complete with horns — one of those plastic ones from a toy shop, thought Billy. As he watched in amusement, the guest blew out the candle in front of him and ate it. His friend, who wore a more extravagant set of horns and who sat head and shoulders above the others, turned to him, scowling. Billy felt some sympathy for the first Viking — there was nothing on the table but water and candles and it was almost midnight.

Up and down the table Billy searched for his customer. There was a row of guests whose faces he could not see, the ones with their backs to the window. Most of the backs were wearing fur coats, like the woman at the head.

Ah — there was the builder — standing up at the other end of the table, his battered felt hat firm on his head and one hand resting on its brim. A woman smaller than the builder but bearing a strong family resemblance — his sister, maybe — stood beside him, her hand resting also on her own hat, a grey and white cloche. The table fell silent, all heads turned to watch them. Swiftly, elegantly, the couple removed their hats to reveal, springing from each head, a pair of long, furry, pink-lined ears. Below the ears the faces now blurred, took new shapes: he was a hare and she was a rabbit.

Dumbstruck, Mack and Billy watched as the metamorphosis continued around the table: the first fur-coated woman was nothing but an opossum, destroyer of forests and coastal trees.

What Billy had previously taken to be an ornate chair back was in fact her bushy tail. The spiky-haired man twinkled now all over with the spines of a hedgehog; the mother wallaby beside him soothed her agitated joey with her paws. Beside her sat not her husband, but a mynah bird, preening and vain. Further along was the lonely depressive, a ship rat. A poplar tree, a willow, a goat and deer were next, the goat still chomping his mouthful of candle, white globules of wax shining in his whiskers. Great hilarity erupted around the table when all the changes were complete — there was wild and extensive toasting, evident delight in one another's appearance.

Billy's one-time customer rang a glass.

'My friends, it is with the greatest of pleasure that I welcome you to my house.' His voice was loud and high and carried easily to the brothers' ears. 'You are safe here — no guns can trace us, no traps, poisoned bait or native-garden enthusiasts. Is it our fault we were transported to this country?'

It was a rhetorical question, but a resounding negative rose from all sides.

'And do we intend to stay?'

'Absolutely!' supplied the goat, scraping at his whiskers with a hoof.

'This very site, my friends,' the hare went on, 'was intended for the construction of a five-star hotel, a cinema complex, a golf course and a games parlour. Better by far for Mother Earth that it be our refuge. A crown of thorns adorns a nearby hill, beds of hay and soft earth await your dreaming heads in the . . .' He paused, as if trying to remember a word, '. . . sleep-out. We are innocent creatures, taking root, crawling and walking upon the innocent earth.'

A great rustling of leaves, snickering, braying and whistling erupted, accompanied by a strong perfume of jasmine, of ginger-plant and morning glory. Only the rat sat quietly, the black end of his nose waffling and scenting at the air. Suddenly he stood up on his hind legs, his mouth open in a kind of rat-bark, his long worm tail lashing behind him. One of his pink hands pointed at the shadowy faces on the other side of the glass.

'Let's go!' Billy looked at his brother. They'd been crouched there for so long that Billy's bad knee had seized up like a rusty padlock.

Eyes shining, a childish, delighted grin on his face, Mack stood up.

'No!' Billy made a lunge to stop him — his brother was opening the door — but his knee crumpled and he landed hard on the boards.

He didn't think he'd knocked his head as he went down, but he must have — and judging by the time of day, he'd been out to it for some time. The builder sat in his chair on the verandah, the beer and glasses beside him. Billy sat up.

'Where's Mack?' he asked.

'Who?' the builder asked softly.

'My brother — I followed him up here last night —'

The builder shook his head. 'I'm sorry, I haven't seen him. But you — I opened my door this morning and there you were, dead drunk and curled up on the verandah.'

'But I —'

'Hair of the dog?' offered the builder, with a glimmer of humour in his dark brown eyes.

A sudden, terrible thirst gripped Billy by the throat and he drank the proffered glass, down to the very last drop. Then, without saying goodbye, he staggered along the bluff for home and a good long sleep.

'I had the weirdest bloody dream of my life,' said Mack that afternoon, as they were getting ready to go fishing.

'Yeah?' asked Billy carefully. 'What about?'

'Introduced animals. Yeah, that's what they were. Pests.'

'What were they doing?' Billy asked casually, throwing a plastic bag of frozen bait into the boat.

'Shit . . . it's kind of embarrassing. It was a kids' dream. They were all up there —' He pointed at the grove of trees surrounding the finished house, 'having one hell of a party.'

Mother Maryam

One of the questions Rick is asked, now that he trawls celebrity-style through his fifteen minutes of fame, is 'How did she think she would get away with it?' Just now journalists are not allowed anywhere near me, which is a shame because I could answer the question directly then. Quite often, lying here on my bed, I imagine what I would say to them if they were allowed in; what I would say if they asked *me* that question; how I would explain where the inspiration came from, what my true feelings are, whether I suffer any regrets. I would be ordered in my telling of the tale; not like Rick, who seems to leap about all over the shop and can only talk about his own responses to the situation, not mine. He doesn't even seem to know what our kids think about it. Very often, on the sound bites I've managed to catch before the nurses come running and herd me away from the Dayroom, Maryam is sitting beside him nodding sagely, though I suspect her understanding of the conversation around her is minimal.

If I was asked, I'd begin with the idea and where it came from. I'd begin like this, like a story:

Inspiration of any kind is not what you expect in Pak'N Save but inspired I was, a year ago, while I was shunting a trolley massive with pesticides, herbicides, modified genes and wordy coloured plastic. At the end of the aisle, examining bags of flour and sugar, stood two North African Muslim women. They were heavily veiled in flocked, fine velvet, their dresses voluminous and dark. In profile only their hands, foreheads and feet showed skin, a glint of gold on the hands, the sandals high-heeled and feminine, toenails boudoir red.

I stopped beside them, hunting for icing sugar. As one of the women weighed a bag of flour in her narrow hands, the other dragged out a five kg sack and hoisted it into their trolley. It seemed they were discussing the purchase and agreeing to take the larger bag. Afterwards they moved off, heads together, side by side at the trolley handle, and I didn't catch sight of them again until I joined the queue at the checkout. The one who hoisted the bag was now heaving out all the shopping and the other was standing a little to one side with her hands folded on her long dress — her jilbab — resting over her pregnant stomach. Above the veil her eyes were soft and dreamy, her forehead a smooth, brown blaze in the high fluorescent light. The one doing all the work was older, perhaps in her late thirties or early forties, her eyes crow's-footed and her framed expanse of brow faintly scored with three or four lines.

In the carpark, I saw them join a man who waited with a child asleep in the back seat. Bored, he stayed slumped at the wheel, picking his teeth, while the women filled the boot.

As I passed by them, the true relationship of those women

broke over me like a wave: it was as real and engulfing as if they had looked up from their boot-packing and told me: 'We are his wives.' It was as if they had told me how together they cooked, cleaned, bore and raised children, took turns in his bed. As I passed them the younger one reached out to lie for a moment the flat of her hand on the other's labouring back, a gesture of affection and concern.

On the way home I thought about them, the lives they must lead. I saw them side by side at the kitchen bench, weighing beans. I saw them folding an overwhelming basket of laundry. I saw how the younger one managed the hoovering while the older one helped the children with their homework; how they planned celebratory meals together; how they dealt with headlice, flu and stomach-bugs. One was better at baking, the other at the erotic arts.

And always, always, always, they had company. They didn't spend the hours alone in the house that I do, wielding a desultory toilet-brush, flicking about an ineffectual duster, waiting for the phone to ring and listening to the silence.

It wouldn't be bad, I thought, having another wife around to help shoulder the burden of the house, the kids and Rick. And if she added another baby to the family, that would be fine too. I always wanted more, and now that I'm nearly fifty I'm too old. Another wife would free me up considerably for other things: intellectual pursuits, some serious drinking and afternoon sleeps.

I've always known I'm prone to depression, I would tell the journalists, but now I suspect I'm also obsessive, because once an idea has taken hold of me I find it hard to let go. At the time I made the decision to find Rick and me another wife, the black dog had my throat in his jaws and now and again gave me a shake discombobulating enough to keep me in my bed. In fact, my trip to Pak'N Save came about only because the children had had takeaways for tea three nights running. The guilt had got to me.

People imagine depression to be banal and somehow calm, still, dead water, idle — because that's how it often presents. Not so. True depressives are people with overactive minds. Behind the orbs of our melancholic eyes, self-regarding and febrile fantasies vie with a refusal to accept the dreary, quotidian facts of human existence. For me, once the depression lifts and the black dog moves on to hound someone else, the obsessive idea becomes the likeliest plan of action and I am incapable of subjecting it to any rational examination.

I began the process on the 3rd of May and by Christmas we had her. It was far quicker and easier than I would have thought. Rick is telling the truth when he says he had no clue what I was up to, not until he discovered her tucked up in his duvet when he fell, heavily sauced, into bed on Christmas Eve. Of course, he'd known I'd moved Jimmy into the games room, his bed jammed between the wall and the billiard table, and Stevie in to share with Luke, and that for a month or so I'd been doing out Jimmy and Stevie's old room, stripping it of their posters, soccer boots, mouldy socks and abandoned experiments. I'd put in a king single — I had, after all, slept in a double bed for twenty-two years and an ordinary single would have been too much of an adjustment — and painted the walls a waiting, innocuous cream. She and I would slowly fill it with personal objects required on our off-nights — books, CDs, chocolates, a small fridge stocked with wine and rare, expensive delicacies.

Another of the questions Rick is asked, as he continues to trawl celebrity-style through his fifteen minutes of fame, is if I had ever said I was surprised when I first saw her, if I had got cold feet, if at that stage I had finally questioned my motives and the morality of the situation. He always says he doesn't know, that you'd think after two decades with the same woman you'd know the workings of her mind, but that he obviously didn't, though he'd thought he did. He suspected something was up, he told the sympathetically nodding heads of Paul Holmes and John Campbell and even David Letterman; he said he remembered asking me if I was having an affair.

The truth is, I was so far down the track by the time Maryam arrived, I could never have turned back even if I'd had some niggling doubts, which I didn't. I felt only, as Maryam first became visible on the giant screen in the Arrivals Hall, a great sense of achievement, as I imagine the buyers in my husband's Greenlane car yard do when they're persuaded to purchase an Audi, a Beamer, a Porsche — some cock-car far beyond their means but full of potential adventure.

Maryam was at least as beautiful as her prototypes, the women I'd seen choosing flour. Her face, seen for the first time close up, showed an habitual dreaming calm, a deep acceptance of all the injustices and difficulties of her life. I know this will be hard for you understand, but within moments of meeting her, I wished I *was* her. I wanted to have had her experiences, for my face to be like hers, not with its bitter lines around the corners of its mouth, its perpetual irritable scowl. She seemed more real than I was.

The last ten years of Maryam's life, prior to flying to New Zealand, had been of unremitting hardship and poverty in an Iranian refugee camp in Turkey. All the men in her family are dead — not a male survives over the age of nine. She came to us through our local church, which is an American one with powerful connections in the rescuing business. Here I could go into detail about the paperwork, the money I paid out, the people

I bribed both here and some outfit on the internet which somehow also got involved — but I've been asked not to do that. Immigration was alarmed at how easy it was for me to get her, our sweet, uncomplaining Maryam. It wouldn't be so easy now, not since the war.

I carried her bag for her to the car and we drove to a motel in St Heliers, not far from our place, a couple of blocks towards the water. I had been there earlier in the day to stock the kitchenette with food and stack the table with dictionaries and simple readers filched from Stevie's school-bag. It seemed reasonable to me that she have at least a primitive grasp of English before she came to live with us. On top of the books was a photo album, so that she could acquaint herself with the faces of her new family. I showed her how to operate the remote control, how the kettle worked, and left her to sleep off her jet lag. She wasn't happy about me leaving her at first, but after a while the doctored tea I gave her dried up her tears and put her on the nod. I pulled the covers over her and drove home.

Every day for nearly a month I spent hours with her, perfecting her for Ricky Dicky. It was a time of utter bliss: I was consumed with excitement and anticipation. (No wonder the poor man thought I was having an affair!) Her English came along in fits and starts and she learned to cook some of Rick's favourite meals as far as was possible in the under-equipped kitchen. At first, she was frightened of me. I suppose she disliked being locked in each evening as I left, and sometimes I had to force her to have her tea so that she would be quiet until I came back again, though she never did cry out or try to draw attention to herself.

I assuaged my conscience by telling myself women like her are often confined, that after all these centuries they must have a genetic predisposition to it, a kind of innate anti-claustrophobia. I took her soiled laundry home and brought it back clean, secretly attending to it while the family were out at work or school; I made sure she always had enough to eat and was warm and comfortable. My only worry was that she would fall sick and I would have to take her to a doctor. If that happened, I planned, I'd go somewhere in Manukau City, somewhere chaotic and impoverished, somewhere where an overworked doctor might not ask too many questions.

It was during the week before Christmas that Rick's Christmas present made her first visit to the house, the house that has since been photographed and splashed all over every newspaper and news show in the country. A month ago Rick put it on the market; because of its infamy and views it's bound to fetch about a million. She liked the Spanish arches around the front entrance, the yukkas in the beds of stones, the retro shagpile in the games room and Luke's Persian cat. She touched all those things, and asked me for the word for them. She dipped her hand in the swimming pool and would have taken a mouthful of it, but I stopped her. The view from the picture window in the dining room, over the roofs to the harbour, transfixed her.

'Sea,' she said, pointing. 'Boats.' Above her face-veil her eyes crinkled, the skin around them pushed upwards by her curtained smile.

Her response to the kitchen disappointed me. I thought she'd be pleased to see all the things I'd shown her pictures of in the brochures I'd taken to the motel, brochures I'd held on to since I'd bought the things years ago: the breadmaker, the dishwasher, the blender, the espresso machine, even the fridge and stove. She showed no desire to push any of the buttons, even though I'd given her rudimentary lessons in their operation.

Instead she brought her hand up to her face, slipping it under her niqab, and stifled a bored yawn.

The piano in the family room elicited more of a response — she pressed down several keys at once and listened carefully as the unharmonious chord jangled through the open-plan, harmonious-flow part of the house. She brought her left hand to join her right and explored the lower reaches, but the bass notes seemed to alarm her and she sprang away, hurried down the little flight of steps to the games room. I watched her take in Jimmy's bed, the billiard table — she picked up a shiny white ball, carressed it, replaced it on the baize — but it was my exercycle that interested her more.

Hooking her long dress into her knickers, she hoisted herself up, carefully placed her feet on the pedals and pedalled, slowly at first, then faster and faster, her lap a padded cushion of pumping, piled-up frock. I fancied she was smiling a little under her niqab, her eyes incandescent, black as treacle in the light diffused through my white nets, and I decided right then to buy her one of her very own for Christmas. We could come here in the late afternoons, face west to the gilding hills as the sun set and race away together, side by side, sweating a little, pumping on the moss-green Bremworth. Even though by then I had begun to suspect that Maryam wasn't the full quid, that her simplicity somehow went beyond her peasant, refugee past, it never occurred to me that I should give her up. I thought we would get along just fine. I would have remained loyal to the contract.

I never did get to see her on her exercycle, though I had bought it and hidden it in the garage, wrapped in swathes of bright paper. I was gone by the time she opened it, taken away on Christmas Eve, just after midnight.

At eleven o'clock on the 24th of December I was in the

kitchen, drying up the last of the dishes, when Rick emerged from his bedroom, his hair tousled, an intensely puzzled and somehow panicked expression on his face. After talking to me for a while, during which time his alarm vanished, to be replaced by what I call his salesman's voice, a sing-song decisiveness, he rang the services.

'My wife has lost her mind,' I heard him say into the cordless, and I thought then of my cellphone in my bag and how I wished I could ring someone — but who? I could text the Minister of Immigration and try to make him understand that having Maryam to live with us was a two-way act of charity. But I couldn't move; I felt turned to stone, my back wedged into the kitchen bench and a damp tea-towel over my shoulder.

With Maryam up and dressed and all her paperwork that Rick could gather from the hall stand, my top drawer and handbag assembled on the table, we waited quietly for other people to arrive. It was the only time we were all three knowingly alone together — though I'd been revelling in the thought privately all night since I'd gone to fetch her, ostensibly to the wine shop for some chardonnay. I'd snuck her in through the internal garage to the laundry, out the back door, up the side path and through the bedroom window. Never at any stage did she offer resistance; she showed no maidenly fear of her imminent intimacy with my husband — but then she was no virgin, our Maryam.

One day at the motel she pointed at a photograph of me, young and milky, holding Stevie. She pointed at herself then, and mimicked rocking a baby in her arms.

'I have baby,' she said. 'Son. In Turkey.'

Now, I believe, Rick is making arrangements for her son to join them. We would never have become a cause célèbre if he hadn't fallen in love. That last part of the story I can't comment on, but it might be enough to get me out of here. If Rick accepts this wife and puts me away from him, then he has accepted that I did at least in part the right thing; that I have provided a future for him, even though he no longer wants me personally to be a part of it. It's because of me he's got Maryam.

The only one of the kids I've seen lately is Jimmy, Rick having decided that as he's nearly sixteen he's old enough to decide if he wants to witness his mother in the nuthouse or not. Jimmy tells me it's all in my mind, that Rick is not marrying Maryam now or ever, that he's just taken on some of the responsibility for helping her to stay here, now that she is here, and to have her son with her.

But I don't believe him.

Most of the time I just lose myself in my parallel life, the life that still goes on in my head, and perhaps also out there in the wealthy, placid eastern suburbs above the sea. In my favourite scene, one I return to again and again, Rick and I lie glistening with oil on our banana beds while Jimmy and Stevie and Luke run in a circle in the pool, setting up a whirligig they can surf on, briefly, before running again, the water swirling in a froth of chlorine and strong, tanned, young legs — and always, in this particular fantasy, on a spinning green flutterboard in the centre of their surging circle, is a fat brown baby sitting upright and cross-legged, gurgling and chortling, smacking the water with his fists, while a sleek head breaks the surface and Maryam swims towards her son, rolling onto her back with her face lifted to the sky and she's laughing, and so are Rick and I and every single one of our trinity of sons.

Maximum Turnover

Her stiletto heels had jammed between two slats of the barbecue table. Yes, that must have been what happened. One moment she was spinning in the chill night air, kicking off the caterer's plates, the red flare of her skirt billowing around her skinny thighs, one pale-nippled breast breaking free from her low-cut Lycra evening top, the hem of that top twisting and tightening at her waist, the glass beads her mother had given her as a going-away present flying out and catching her under the chin — then the next moment she was falling, graceless, arching, catching her spine on the rough edge of the bench seat.

The skin on her back was stinging and there was a long, hot, jagged pain down one of her legs which pulsed once, twice, three times — had she severed a nerve, or a vein? — the pulsing in time with the beat of the music from inside, with the looping swinging of the tree that shaded the table, in time with the swaying of the giant flaming mushroom that was the patio heater and the rhythmic sharpening and softening of the edges of the silhouettes of other guests. She put her head between her knees.

After a moment the world steadied and she stood up, carefully, smoothing down her clothes. Luckily no one had seen, or so it seemed, though surely some people might have — hadn't she been the focus of the party when she was table-dancing? Had they all turned away just before she fell? Certainly nobody was looking at her now, least of all Leonard, the host, the frosty bisexual architect, who hours ago now had opened the door to her with a sneering curl to his upper lip.

'You on your own?' he'd asked, looking behind her for her friend Amber, whom he disliked possibly even more than he did Chelsea.

'Yup,' she'd said, opening her hand and showing him the little white pills, three of them as promised, standing on their edges in the crevice of her palm. Leonard let her in, taking the E from her.

'Pay you later,' he said.

He still hadn't. She could see him, on the other side of the open-plan living room, on his tiptoes to kiss a newcomer, a tall blonde with a red mouth and flashing teeth.

One of the heels was snapped in half. She took off both of her shoes and threw them into the yuccas and ferns of Leonard's professionally landscaped garden. There was a thud as they struck the dry-stone wall behind the plants, loud enough to make a guy sitting on his own under the patio heater look up. She smiled at him. He was good-looking in a boring, businessman kind of way, in a sports jacket no one wore any more who wasn't over sixty, a maroon shirt and a bad haircut.

'You all right?' he asked.

'Why wouldn't I be?'

'You just fell off the table.'

'I'm okay.' She took a step towards him and felt the muscles in her back move raw skin against the prickly, sparkly fabric of her top. 'Maybe I've got a graze.'

'Maybe.'

'You a friend of Leonard's?'

'Went to school with him years ago.'

She smiled again, feeling dizzy. Had she banged her head? She didn't think so.

'What about you?' the man asked.

'I'm Chelsea.'

He smiled now, for the first time. He had a nice mouth, soft and cushiony.

'And? You're here why?'

'Oh, I delivered some happy pills. I'm the courier.'

'Yeah?' The man looked around behind him, across the deck and through the glass that formed the northern wall of Leonard's house. The host was standing with a group of men. None of them was talking — the music was too loud.

'Tell him Blake'd like one.'

'You look too straight for that kind of thing, Blake.' She touched his jacket.

'Not at all. Has the same effect on me as anyone else. Makes me interested in people who'd otherwise bore me shitless.'

'Like me, for instance?' She poked her hip out at him, wiggled her arse. Why would she want him to like her? she wondered. He reminded her of teachers at school, those memories still fresh, only two years old. She met his eyes. They were hard, appraising. And brown, she thought, leaning closer. Or possibly green.

'So how does Leonard know you?'

'Through my friend Amber. Her and Tip, her boyfriend. Tip's a cook, you know.' She waggled her eyebrows. It was hard to tell how old Blake was. She supposed he was Leonard's age, if they'd gone through school together. Somewhere around thirty.

'So what do you do?' Blake asked her; wearily, she thought, as if he was following a script. 'For a job?'

'This and that. Whatever pays the rent.'

'So you've got somewhere we could go?'

He was quick, quicker than her. She'd only just got the idea.

'Yeah. You got a car?'

'Not here.'

'We'll get a cab.'

For a moment he looked as though it was all too difficult and he couldn't be bothered, but then he sighed and stood up.

'Come on, then,' he said, not looking at her, jamming his hands in his pockets.

On the other side of the glass wall the guests had started dancing. At Leonard's parties no one ever danced in couples because Leonard detested people who came in pairs. It was like passing through an arrangement of life-size jiggle toys, those plastic figures strung with elastic that flopped and bounced when you depressed the button in the base. These jigglers were penguins, perhaps, or seals, all in black. Some of the dancers had their eyes closed.

Outside, away from the patio heater, it was cold. A sou'easterly sliced up the gully from the motorway, fumy and watery. From down near the flyover a supermarket bag billowed end over end up the street towards them. It passed by determinedly, white and crackling, as if it knew where it was going — which was more than Chelsea did. Lots of girls did this just once or twice, she knew; they didn't necessarily do it again. Besides, it couldn't be all that bad because the Prime Minister, who was a woman, had made it legal, made it a career path. Chelsea didn't think of it like that, though: it was just a quick solution if you were in a tight spot, like she was. Amber wasn't talking to her because Tip had given her a smack in the eye for helping herself to his gear, which had all been Chelsea's idea. He'd threatened to cut off Amber's hands, like that samurai sword guy did to his girlfriend, if she didn't get the money back — or the gear, he didn't mind which. Whatever came first. The stuff she'd sold to Leonard was the last of what they'd nicked.

Bugger it. She'd forgotten to get the money off him. She'd have to come back later.

'Might have more luck if we go up onto Great North Road.' She began to walk away from him. Maybe this was a bad idea. Maybe it'd be safer and wiser just to stop in a doorway somewhere; maybe he wouldn't fancy walking too far and want to go back inside to the party.

'Hey.' He was beside her. 'You really taking me somewhere, or what?'

'We could go down there if you like.' She pointed down an alleyway that ran between a panelbeater's and a video shop. 'Thirty dollars.'

Was that the right amount? Too much? Not enough? She watched him closely. It was beginning to rain properly now — a droplet landed on his eyelid, hung quivering on a lash before it fell, striping his cheek like a tear. He wiped it off, shook his head.

'Nope. You take me where you take . . . whoever.'

'Okay.' She patted him on the arm, soothingly. He seemed agitated. 'Okay — up here.' She took his hand and led him up the hill.

A taxi came along just as they reached the corner. There was a picture of Krishna on the dashboard and a smell of cigarettes and incense, or a heavy, flowered oil. Beside her in the back seat he sat quietly, looking out at the passing wet streets. The time had passed for her to find out any more about him. That opportunity had been at the party. What do you do? she could have asked him. Are you married? Kids? Got a girlfriend? How much do real hookers ask for?

'You got any cash on you?' She supposed that was the most important question. It was her father's genes coming out in her — he was always good at collecting his debts. She pictured him at home now, in his big house above the sea, watching TV with his new wife and the twins. No — the twins would be in bed by now. She pictured them in their Winnie-the-Pooh-theme bedroom, their little cheeks flecked by the rain shadows on the window, the bears and Piglets and Roos swinging on mobiles and pinned to the walls, the soft hum of the air-conditioning. Suddenly, over the incense and stale cigarette pong, there was the smell of the twins after their baths, the crisp scent of their laundered pyjamas, their healthy skins and shiny hair, the privilege of their perfumed childhoods. Hers had been like that too, with a loving mother tucking her in every night. Her father's absence hadn't bothered her as much as it was supposed to, if you believed all the stuff about fatherless girls.

She crossed her legs, lifted Blake's nearest hand and brought it to lie in her lap. It was heavy and damp from more than just the rain. Was he nervous? Maybe he hadn't done this before either. He seemed trustworthy, kind of sad and honest. Maybe it would be safe to take him back to her flat. Amber would be around at Tip's place, doing whatever he or his mates asked of her, to keep him sweet. She would be waiting for Chelsea to show with the money. Leaning forward over Blake's motionless hand she gave the cabby her address in Avondale.

The people in one of the flats downstairs were having a party — there was a line of young men sitting on the low wall outside the building, swigging mixes. One of them offered a newly opened KGB to Chelsea as she went past.

'Merry Christmas,' he said, though it wasn't. It was June.

'Cheers.' She swallowed half of it in one go while Blake paid the driver. She'd got out as soon as the cab had drawn to a halt so he'd had to come up with the fare. Maximum turnover, she thought, that's what was required from this enterprise.

He followed her up the stairs.

'Where'd you get that from?' he asked, when she set the bottle down to rummage in her bag for the keys.

She pointed through the floor towards the origin of the beat that thumped up through the boards.

'Haven't you had enough?'

"S'worn off.'

The door opened into the small, windowless living room that doubled as Chelsea's bedroom. Her sleeping bag and pillow were heaped up on the small foam sofa, which was ripped, showing its crumbling yellow insides. Clothes swirled on the floor in coloured curds, crumpled tissues glowed white, the gold of an empty cigarette packet gleamed in the light from the bulb at the top of the stairs. A poster of J-Lo had come loose from its blu-tak and curled halfway up her semi-naked torso.

There was a faint mewing and Amber's kitten Matrix picked his way across the room.

'Bit of a mess,' Chelsea said apologetically, not looking at him, picking up the kitten.

'Stinks,' Blake agreed.

Her bladder was bursting, but she didn't want to leave him in case he turned around and left, in case he went back down the stairs and out into the night, taking his wallet with him. Matrix wriggled in her hands and she put him down again.

In a jar on an upturned carton beside the sofa was a candle. She lit it and undressed quickly.

'Where are we going to . . .' he said, one foot on her black T-shirt, the one that had glittery letters on it that said 'I'M WORTH IT'.

'Here.' She spread the sleeping bag over the sofa, straightened the pillow and lay down, her eyes on the candle. It was flickering and jumping in time to the beat from the downstairs party, which reminded her of something — a TV ad for a herbicide from when she was a kid, Round-Up was it, which had thistles that danced just like that, nodding their shaggy heads . . .

His shoes hit the floor, she heard his zip, heard the rustle of his trousers, his footsteps. He lay down half on the narrow squab, half on top of her, his upper body still clothed in shirt and jacket.

'You'll have to show a bit more interest than that.'

She remembered an instruction from something — a leaflet on sex education, was it? — or maybe she'd read it on the back of a Durex packet. *Incorporate the application of the condom into your foreplay.*

'You got a condom?' she asked. Two birds with one stone, then.

He sighed, got up again and went to his trousers. She watched him closely this time as he opened his wallet, like a man searching for the correct change for a parking machine, the same degree of indifferent concentration.

'Give it to me,' she said softly when she saw the flash of silver foil.

She helped him with it, rolled it on, murmured things she

thought he'd like to hear, things gleaned from years of watching late-night TV.

'Mmm, you're a big boy, ain't ya, looking good, uh-huh, sweet as, give it here, ooo can't wait, honey, what a big boy you are —'

'Cut the American accent,' he said, surprisingly. But she wasn't offended. She lay back and hoped he'd be quick.

While he did it, she thought about Amber and how pleased she'd be to get the money and how life would go back to how it was before, the good times they had had, the drinking and smoking dak, the odd tab of acid, a bit of E. Lately Amber had been smoking P out of a pipe Tip had given her. Crank was where Chelsea drew the line.

'That's crazy stuff,' she'd said. 'It just brings you down and makes you mean.'

Blake had stopped suddenly, without making any noise. Was he finished already? She wasn't going to ask.

He stood up, pulled on his undies and trousers.

'You enjoy your work?' he asked, she thought perhaps sarcastically.

"S'all right. You enjoy yours?'

He sat on the edge of the sofa to do up his shoes. She looked down at them for long enough to see the kitten shit on the toe of one of them, and looked away again.

'Do you?' she persisted. She felt pissed off with him suddenly, with herself, with everything. 'What do you do?' She wanted to know now. All she had ever read or heard about men who went with prostitutes had it that they came from every walk of life — married, single, rich, poor. Maybe he was a professional like Leonard. Maybe he was a doctor or a lawyer.

'I'm a plumber,' he said, 'in New Plymouth.'

'That's where I'm from,' she said, before she could stop herself.

'Yeah? What's your name again?'

'Doesn't matter.' What if he went around to fix her mother's sink or something? 'I know your daughter,' he might say. 'I met her in Auckland. She's a filthy little hooker.'

The sex had made her full bladder sting. She couldn't hold on a moment longer. Sitting up, she pulled the sleeping bag around her, like a slippery, puffy cloak.

'Wait a moment,' she said, picking her way across the littered carpet and down a short hall to the bathroom. In the silence that followed the last of the gushing water she heard the door to the flat open and shut. He'd gone. The bastard had done a runner.

Sleeping bag dumped in a puddle from the leaking shower-box, she was out of the bathroom and into Amber's room, which had windows that gave out onto the road. There he was on the other side, striding through the rain, his shining head and sports jacket shoulders moving from one pool of street-light to another, late-night traffic roaring and slicking in the wet between them. Kneeling on Amber's bed, she pushed the window out on its hinges — it could only open a few centimetres — squeezed her face into the narrow gap and yelled after him.

'You! Over there! Effing come back and give me my effing money!'

He disappeared around the corner and the last shreds of the bravado that had buoyed her up all night went with him. Stumbling over Amber's boots and clothes, her arms locked around her stomach, colliding with the shitty, crumbling walls, she made her way back to the sofa and collapsed on it face down, her chest heaving. Maybe she was going to be sick, toss up the KGB and all the wine she'd drunk at Leonard's. There wouldn't be anything else. She hadn't eaten since yesterday.

Something sticky and cold glued itself to her knee. She sat up again, peeled it off — the condom, full of spoof. He had come then. She'd wondered. She flung it away and was about to lie down again when her eye was drawn to the candle, which had burnt down below the lip of the jar. In the gentle light, on the carton, there was a sheen of green and blue. She lunged for it. Two twenties and a ten.

You see, she told herself, in the motherly voice she reserved for the rare occasions she saw the twins, you see? You were right. He was an honest guy. He didn't rip you off.

She dressed and left the flat, the fifty dollars tucked into her purse. Downstairs a carload was heading into town and she got a lift with them. She'd go back to Leonard's and get the money, she decided, then go around to Tip's and make everything all right. On the way they passed Blake, still walking fast, his hair glued to his head with rain, and she waved at him from her perch on some guy's knee, but he didn't see her.

You'll Sleep With No Other

Once there was a blank. As blanks often are, it was white. It was propped up on two wooden legs, and was very bored with itself and everything around it. Especially the five lanes that roared in front of it and gave it a headache.

One day two men and a woman parked a blue van on the grass verge. They unloaded ladders, some buckets of paste, and several large cylinders of paper. The woman leaned a ladder against the blank with a loud thud.

'Ouch,' said the blank, but nobody heard it.

The woman began to slop paste onto the blank with a paintbrush. The blank sighed. The day was very hot and the glue very cool, if a little sticky. After a while the woman climbed down and moved her ladder along. One of the men pushed up a ladder where hers had been. Thunk.

'Ow,' said the blank. But nobody heard.

The man unfurled a long piece of paper and pounded it very firmly so it stuck. Below him the other man pasted and pounded other bits of paper. The blank was slowly disappearing.

'Am I dying?' it thought.

Eventually all three packed away the ladders and the glue and stood back to admire their work. They'd made a picture of a beautiful young man, stretched out as if he'd just woken up.

'Pretty, isn't he?' said one of the men.

Then the blue van drove away.

'Hello,' said the blank, a bit muffled.

'Hello,' said the beautiful young man. 'Where am I?'

'Don't ask me,' said the blank. 'I've asked before myself, but nobody hears me.'

'Who am I, then?' asked the young man.

'You?' asked the blank. 'Don't ask me. I don't even know who I am.'

Then the blank was silent. The young man looked at his downy arms and dark brown nipples in his hairless chest and realised he was beautiful. He felt his legs under the sheet and knew he was strong. His penis pressed hard against the linen, making a little tent. Around him the traffic screamed, and people walked in and out of their houses on the other side of the five lanes.

Presently two girls dressed the same came and stood underneath him. They were in school uniform, but the man wasn't to know that. He'd never been to school.

'Look at that,' said one girl, who had silver bars glinting on her teeth. 'Isn't he a spunk?'

'Yeah,' said the other girl. She scurried around behind the blank.

'She's lighting a cigarette,' said the blank, trembling slightly. 'I hope she doesn't set us on fire.'

The young man didn't reply. Through half-closed eyes he was examining the remaining girl. She was staring up at him with a look on her face that made his penis lie down flat again. The other girl reappeared.

'I think he's fucking beautiful,' breathed the girl with the metal mouth.

'Yeah,' said the other girl, breathing smoke.

'He's a prince,' said the first girl.

'Yeah,' said the smoking girl. 'Wouldn't you like to meet the real thing, but?'

They laughed and the metal mouth flashed. They walked on, smoke curling around their heads.

'The real thing?' asked the young man. 'I am the real thing.'

'She told you what you are, anyway,' said the blank.

'What was that?'

'A prince,' said the blank. 'I must say, it's awfully hot under you.'

'Prince of what?' asked the young man.

But the blank was silent.

Later, just before sundown, a very old swallow flew by. She perched on top of the blank and panted.

'I am a prince,' said the young man.

'Uh huh,' said the swallow, which was all she could manage.

'What am I prince of?' asked the young man.

'Everything you can see around you,' replied the swallow, and flew off.

The young man swivelled his eyeballs around. For three days and three nights he watched and learned. Through the windows of the houses opposite he saw people eating and making love. He saw them sitting in front of mirrors taking black shadows off their faces, or reddening their pursed lips with pink sticks. He saw children sitting at tables laden with food, screaming for an alternative.

On the third day two women stopped. One glanced at him. 'Turn you on?' she said.

'I think it's disgusting,' said the other woman, bending to her bootlaces. 'I think it's consumerist sexism.'

'Well, at least the boys are doing it to each other,' replied the first woman. 'No need to graffiti this one.'

'What's he advertising?' asked the bootlace woman, straightening up.

'Who cares?' said the first woman, taking the other's arm, leading her off.

'Consumerist sexism? Advertising? What's that?' asked the young man, baffled.

At least the young man now knew he was the Prince of Sensuality, where people walked about draped in satin sheets eating avocado with their fingers; and Prince of Vanity, where there were so many mirrors people often found themselves talking to mere reflections for hours. He knew he was Prince of Plenty, where everybody always wanted more; and Prince of Noise, reigning supreme above the grinding cars, where people talked loudly about nothing and slowly grew deaf.

He could see for miles. He could see over the five lanes, and the pink and yellow terraced houses, and the wattle and clotheslines in the gardens. He could see over the barracks to the golf course. He could see through the smog to the tops of the very tall buildings like tall, rich ladies, ugly with flashing diamond lights and grimy pearls. And beyond he could see the Blue Mountains, far off. The young man knew that the mountains meant the boundary of his kingdom. He wondered if they were in fact another prince. A prince so huge that he was distinguishable all around the edge of the city. This other prince did not seem to move much except for inching a little closer on fine days. The young man wasn't worried. He couldn't move any more than an eyeball either, and even then only very discreetly.

All day every day he lay stretched out on the cream bed, his naked torso open to the grey-streaked rain or blistering sun. Above his sleepy mouth and just visible tongue dangled a bunch of purple grapes held at the stalk by a white hand with crimson talons. The hand puzzled the young man. He wondered who it belonged to. Occasionally, when his mouth was dry, he would demand that the grapes be lowered. But the hand remained immobile, the red nails glistening.

Below the young man's bed there was a sentence. The letters marched along, hiccupping at the many exclamation marks and hyphens, but making it to the edge of the blank all the same. The young man wondered what the sentence said.

The summer pounded on. There was a gap when everybody went away, the word 'Christmas' on their lips, avarice in their eyes, and pockets jingling lighter each time they walked past. This was when the young man discovered he was lonely. For a month now the blank had been quiet, as blanks should be. And loneliness was not the young man's only discomfort. He'd noticed his chest was bubbling, little blisters rising and tearing. The sheets were fraying, and although he wasn't sure, the young man felt he was lying on more of a slant than usual. He wondered if his beauty was impaired.

One evening, just before sundown, the young man heard a familiar fluttering. The old swallow had returned. She sat on top of the blank, picking nits from under her wings. He waited for her to speak, to acknowledge his presence. Finally he cleared his throat.

'Don't you remember me?' he asked.

'Mmm,' said the swallow, her head beneath her wing.

'I'm the Prince of Everything I See Around Me,' he continued.

'Mmm,' said the swallow, scratching her chest.

'Um,' said the young man, 'would you do me a favour?'

'If it's quick,' said the swallow.

'I've got a sentence under me. Do you know what it says?'

'A sentence?' said the swallow. 'Once I sat outside a jail and heard them talk about their sentences. Are you in for long?'

'I don't know,' answered the young man. 'Do all princes live in jails?'

'Hang on a tick,' said the swallow, taking flight.

The young man looked down on her beating wings as she followed his sentence along the bottom of the bed.

'It says,' said the swallow on her return, getting ready for the recital, '"Once You've Slept With Prince You'll Sleep With No Other." And underneath that it says "Billboard Enterprises Ltd."'

'But I sleep alone!' said the young man.

'It's a kind of mattress,' said the swallow. 'You're an advertisement.' And flew off.

After that the young man grew sadder and sadder. He hardly noticed when people returned from their holidays and once again the five lanes were clogged with cars.

One morning around dawn, two men walked hand in hand along the road and paused beneath him. They passed a sweet-smelling cigarette between them and looked up at his blistered chest and face.

'He hasn't enjoyed the summer any more than you have, love,' said the man whose turn it was with the sweet cigarette.

'I'll bet his bum isn't as red as mine is,' said the other man, uncomfortable in his tight pants.

'He's become an affront,' continued the first man. 'I rather fancied him when he first went up.'

'Oh — you'd fancy anything up,' said the one with sunburn. He reached up and peeled away a bit of the sentence.

'Once You've Slept With Prince You'll Sleep With No Other,' he chanted and laughed. They embraced, for a long time, breathing through their noses.

Just after sunup it rained. It was the first rain since well before Christmas. With his unblistered eye the Prince watched the people coming out of the houses opposite. They were smiling.

'Thank goodness it's rained,' they said. 'That ought to lower the temperature.'

If his people were glad about it, then he ought to be too, reasoned the Prince, although the rain had weakened the last remaining scrap of paper that held his right arm to his shoulder. While it had previously cushioned his handsome head on the generous pillows, it now drifted about the footpath. The young man watched it disappear under the blank, to be tangled up in the long grass and fraternise with the plastic bags.

When the sun was at its highest, two women and a man pulled up in a blue van with Billboard Enterprises Ltd written on it. They surveyed the Prince.

'Just as well he's got to come down,' said the man. 'He's coming away from the board.'

With that they raised their ladders and began tearing and ripping at the young man.

He commanded them to stop.

He screamed in agony.

But nobody heard him.

After they'd gone, the blank woke up from its long summer sleep.

'. . . into the care of his mother'

Tomorrow morning the Department deliver him up to me — they'll bring him home. Not that he ever lived here, in this poxy house — how many times have I shifted since he went out into the world for the last time? They're bringing him between four and six, while it's still dark, which they have to do, given all the hoo-ha drummed up around his release. I'll get a phone call on their approach.

Bed's made. Did that this afternoon. Three blankets and the spread should keep him warm enough. He'll notice the difference, how much colder it is. Pare's a long way north — a long, long way.

It's coming up 6 pm. Could turn on the telly, see the news — see the concerned residents, see the Corrections Minister defend the court's decision. But I'd rather sit here by the window, look out at the darkening street and think about it all, be thankful

I went to the supermarket as soon as my benefit came through, bought enough food for a week, so that we won't have to go outside. Best we stick in the house, best no one sees his face.

Not sure I want to look at his face.

Not the face he's got now — twenty-nine years old, after eleven years inside. He looks forty, his teeth gone bad, deep lines in his brow. He was a handsome boy, Jared, but he's pissed it away. Father was a looker, too, a brown Casanova with the strongest smoke in Tauranga. Didn't know him long, only a couple of weeks in the fourth form before my family away to another town.

Phone's ringing — but I won't answer it. It'll be that journalist chap again. Certainly won't be any of my four others, born after Jared over the next ten years, all to different dads, all girls and not one of them talking to me, not since some time in the nineties. They like to blame me for the mess their lives are in. They've all been offered counselling for trauma and grief at different times, and the counsellors park it all at my door. After Sheena lost her baby in a house fire, after Kareena got stabbed by her useless boyfriend, after Deirdre was raped by the Mongrel Mob, after Shandra's partner was had up for interfering with one of her kids — all that colossal fucking shit, they told me the counsellors told them, was all my fault.

They don't want me: that's fine. I know I made plenty of mistakes. But nothing'll stop me worrying about them, reeling around out there from one disaster to another, taking my grand-children with them. Least Jared hasn't fathered any.

There's someone knocking at the door.

This evening, Debbie had decided, was the time to deliver the letter and petition. It was leaving it a little late, but there were still some signatures to collect from the other side of town. Nobody wanted him. Nobody at all. The Department wouldn't listen, the government wouldn't listen, the mayor said his hands were tied. Mrs Knowles was the last resort.

She asked her husband drive her, even though it was really only just around the corner, and he said he'd be honoured and that it was great she'd at long last found something she could really commit herself to. He was so proud of her, even staying home from work this morning to give moral support when she was interviewed on *Morning Report*.

'Mothers have to be responsible for their own children,' Debbie told the interviewer. She didn't hold with all this blaming-the-state business. In the end it came down to personal responsibility, and Knowles's mother had to understand that there were a lot of young families with children in the area, that this part of Wanganui had changed now that everyone wanted to be near the river. As Craig said, this whole business was affecting the town's image and could effect a downturn. Craig should know, being the president of the Mainstreet Business Association. It was criminal the way that up until now no one had listened, not even to Craig or anyone from Lions or Rotary.

One bright street-lamp cast a sharp shadow over the little house, a dun-coloured wooden one like the others in the street, but *orig. cond.*, as Craig would advertise it. There were deep cracks in the front path, purple in the fluorescent light with thick moss bulging in them like her own varicose veins, she thought suddenly, anxiety welling as she knocked on the front door.

Craig was watching. She'd keep it short and sweet, hand it over and go. She gave him a brave little wave, just as the door opened a crack. At thigh height an old dog's muzzle protruded, black flecked with grey.

'Yes? Can I help you?'

There was no porch light — the wall fixture was empty. It was hard to see her — grey hair, of course, or was it an ashy blonde? The door opened further and Debbie saw that the woman who stood there was not much older than her. The same age even, in her early forties. She wore cheap cotton half-leg pants, a long black T-shirt, myriad chains around her neck. She had more wrinkles around her mouth than anywhere else — probably a smoker. Big rings in her pink, slightly protuberant ears, two dots tattooed on her cheekbones to say she'd been inside herself: like mother, like son. Debbie's heart sank. Silly, but she'd had an idea in her head that Knowles's mother would be ancient, grey: a mournful old lady. And Maori, since Knowles was. She'd thought she'd be a little old Maori lady. Just as she thrust the papers at her, Craig started up the car, ready to go.

'This is a letter and list of signatures from the residents of our town,' she announced swiftly. 'Read it and please think about what we have to say. Thank you.' And she turned around and strode down the path in her new adidas shoes, which really did put a new spring in her step, the first since the birth of her first child six months ago — that worth-every-penny expensive baby who would now be needing his evening feed.

'Well done, darling,' said Craig as he drove, giving her knee a sweet little pat.

The woman at the door looked like a television cook, like Easy-Peasy or Food in a Minute: the same wedge haircut and creamy chin rolls. Tracksuit pants didn't do a thing for her. She smelt clean, like packaging, as if she spent so much time in places like K-Mart or The Warehouse that she'd taken on a polymer scent.

Drowned Sprat

The hands that delivered the papers were practical, podgy, small moon nails neatly clipped. Inside a little shiny car pulled up at the kerb was a man bent low over the steering wheel, watching, engine running, and when she turned back up the path he leaned across to open her door for her. I didn't wait to see them drive off but carried the letter inside.

'Dear Mrs Knowles,' read the letter, held out under the hall light. 'You cannot help but be aware of the level of anxiety and distress in the community over the arrival of your son. All other avenues explored to prevent this eventuality have been exhausted. We beg you to put yourself in our position and to consider either — even at this late stage — refusing to accept responsibility for the prisoner, or relocating your household elsewhere. Should you select the second option, a small fund to assist would be forthcoming. We beg you to think of this next generation growing up and of their safety. By our calculations the signatures that follow number one thousand and four.' The list was headed by Craig and Debbie Former, with an address about two blocks away, just up the river in a new subdivision.

Maybe that was her that brought this round. That part of town people hardly go outside, all these big new houses jammed on tiny sections, televisions flickering through chinks in the curtains morning and afternoon — even if I'd walked past she would likely have been inside cleaning one of the four bogs it most likely has. No garden but plenty of places to crap.

Well, stuff her. I take the papers over to the fireplace and lay them on the grate, find some matches and set fire to them. At least, that's what I fully intend to do, but just as I light up the match I change my mind. There's bound to be a lot of trouble in the first few weeks Jared's back. What if he's assaulted, accosted? This list of names could be useful. I fold the sheets in half and put them in a kitchen drawer.

What happens, when we drive through these dark, small towns, is that I don't actually see the lights blurring in the rain, one after another, but the grey in the back of the van shifts, ebbs, loses its grip; lets me see the face of the officer sitting opposite. There are three of them and they take turns to sit with me or up the front. Only one drives.

Three of them, returning me to the care of my mother — singular, female, getting on.

Yesterday they sent the priest to me and I asked him to tell me the story of the prodigal son. Except I couldn't remember 'prodigal' properly, struggled a bit with the word, but he got my meaning.

'It's a parable,' he said and he opened his Bible and read it out to me, from St Luke, and there's no mention of the mother. There's a father and a brother, and the brother was fucked off that he's done everything right while the other has 'wasted his substance with riotous living'. Lucky he had any substances to waste, I thought, and would've told the priest that joke, but he was an ancient old bugger and wouldn't've got it. Don't know why they sent him to me — he wasn't going to tell me anything interesting, not until I asked him the story. Then he did.

These fat-arse officers are always hungry, stopping for chips and burgers and shit. Me, I stay in the van; they won't even let me out for a smoke. In Taumarunui some passing dick bangs hard on the roof while we're parked and fuckin' freaks me. Doing well till then.

The old girl won't believe I'm cured, but I am. Not everybody reoffends. In prison I made a survey of it — lots of them weren't priors. I might've fucked up more than once, but I'm finished now. Gonna keep my head down, get a job, earn some money to get out when I can. Get up to Auckland, get a new life, a new name. That's my dream. Possible, no reason. Get a dog, something to love. I'll feed it, keep it close — people who look after things don't get in so much trouble. The screw opposite has a wedding ring that lights up in the towns.

I don't embrace him because of the other men. They stand around, watch him walk up the path towards me on the porch. He's carrying a small bag. I've watched him walk up paths towards me and away from the Services before — how many times? The contents of the bag have changed over the years — teddies to track shoes, Ritalin to Aropax. Who's to know what they've got him on now?

Strange how silent it is. None of the men move or talk. Jared keeps his eyes on the wet path ahead; I watch the men.

'Go now,' I think. One of them steps away from the van, looks up and down the street as if he'd been expecting trouble and can't believe there is none.

We go inside, close the door and look at each other.

'It's going to be all right,' I tell him. I light two ciggies and hand one to him. 'It is, Jared.'

He takes a drag, shakes his head.

'Come in the kitchen.' I take his hand, which is clammy and cold, and lead him to a chair by the heater.

While I get him a beer he sits quiet, though a couple of times he starts to say something, then stops himself.

'Don't rush yourself, pet,' I tell him. 'Take it slow.'

I could talk instead, tell him all the things I never have, like, for instance, how it's not as if I ever made a decision about whether he did it or not; how some days I think he didn't; other days I don't know; but most days I know in my bones that he did. I could tell him that no state of mind is more bearable than any of the others, and that I don't want him to ever try to talk to me about it. I don't want to know.

He drinks his beer, asks for coffee and another cigarette.

'In the drawer,' I say, without thinking. 'There's a whole new packet.'

When I turn to bring him his coffee he's standing by the dresser, reading the letter I got earlier, and the pages of signatures are fluttering in his hand like the wing of a dying bird.

The plan was that a group of about twenty girls from Plunket and Playgroup would meet at Debbie's place before walking around to start the vigil. They were to meet a photographer from the local newspaper outside the Knowles house, who would take their picture, all of them just ordinary normal mums pushing strollers and waving placards.

After she'd provided everyone with morning tea, Debbie led the charge down to the double garage to pick up the signs that she and Craig had painted over the weekend. They leaned on their shafts against the walls, ranged around Craig's boat.

Kerry-Anne's ginger-haired four-year-old came to stand beside her, extending a finger to trace the O of Offender.

'That's for the man that sexed the little girl and killed her dead,' she said solemnly.

'Shsh!' said Kerry-Anne.

'How does she know that?' demanded Debbie. 'Did you tell her?'

'Of course not!' Behind her spectacles Kerry-Anne's pale blue eyes widened defensively.

'I think it's appalling,' Debbie said, 'just appalling that she knows that. You're her mother — you shouldn't let —'

'— TV or radio, one of the older kids —' Kerry-Anne was saying, louder. But Debbie matched her volume.

' — talk about it in front of her. Sponges! Kids are sponges! You're denying her a childhood!'

'What's going on?' It was Tammy, who was young and solo, like Kerry-Anne, and probably just as unskilled at parenting. They lived next door to each other in a block of scruffy units.

'Nothing,' said Debbie.

Kerry-Anne began to cry and her four-year-old joined in.

'For goodness' sake!' said Debbie. She hoisted up a couple of signs and lugged them out to the other mothers, who were gathered outside on the driveway, chatting. 'I could do with a hand,' she told them.

After last night's rain it was still overcast and cold, which made for an invigorating walk down to the Knowles house. Debbie pushed Jared in his buggy, his head a fuzzy blue sphere in his woolly hat. It was most unfortunate he shared his name with the offender — if he'd been born only six months later the shared name could have been avoided. On quite a number of occasions recently she'd wept about it, and she and Craig had had long talks into the night about whether or not they should change Baby's name, even though it was Debbie's favourite even from before they began the fertility treatment. Baby — that's what he was called most of the time, but that couldn't go on forever. Right now he was asleep, a little bubble shining on his lower lip. Poor sweet innocent, thought Debbie, hating suddenly the idea of taking him into close proximity to the monster, close enough to breathe the same air.

The house looked locked up, curtains drawn, a blind pulled

over the frosted glass in the door. No smoke came from the chimney, but Debbie supposed that was because it was a renter and the landlord would have had the fireplace boarded up. Craig advised all landlords to do that, for the fire risk. Too bad if the tenants froze their arses off with no money for the power company. They were lucky, Debbie supposed, that their own house was constructed from completely modern and non-flammable materials, should they ever buy another and rent the first one out. That kind of thing was going on at the moment. An Englishman had come out and bought twenty houses in one swoop to rent out to the locals — a latter-day absentee landlord. Wanganui was definitely going ahead.

'Should we shout things?' one of the mothers asked her.

'I don't think so,' Debbie said. 'This is a silent vigil.'

From the tray under the pram she took the banner and unrolled it. She'd brought string, to attach it to the fence. 'Homicidal Sex Offenders Not Welcome In Our Neighbourhood' it said. Kerry-Anne's sign, 'Murderers Out!', had been painted in the same fluorescent pink.

Once the banner was properly hooked up and the mothers had stopped standing around in groups chatting to stand in a hushed line, the vigil looked serious and important. It was professionally done, thought Debbie, if you could have a professional vigil. She wondered about the woman inside, whether she'd noticed them yet; whether, if she had, she'd pointed them out to her criminal son.

A passing truck tooted at them, a motorcyclist gave them the victory signal as he zipped by, an old couple seated at the bus stop opposite stared at them with astonishment. Debbie wondered if she should go across and explain to them what they were doing — perhaps they didn't even know Jared Knowles was in the house, unrestrained by anyone other than his white-trash mother — but just as she took a step out onto the road the bus came along. When it pulled away the couple looked out the windows at her with a hint of fear on their faces, as if she was somehow more closely associated with the target of the vigil than the spirit of the vigil itself. It gave Debbie a start, and she wondered for the first time if she was doing the right thing. She didn't want any of this to reflect on her and Craig.

'Mrs Former?' It was the photographer, lugging his tripod.

Jared and I are watching them through the nets. They can't see us. We've pulled all the blinds and hooked up blankets and it's like the inside of a cow.

'That's the one that brought the list.' I point out Debbie Former. 'The older one.'

Jared nods and I watch his eyes follow her as she takes pride of place in the pose. The photographer is quick — a couple of shots, then he's back in his car and departing.

The women remain, waving in response to toots from supportive drivers.

'They shouldn't of let me out,' Jared says quietly, his first complete sentence since he got here. He slept for a few hours, but woke suddenly and got up.

'Mum?' he says. 'Should they?'

I wish he was still kipping.

'Mum?'

'Don't know, son.'

'Don't know if I should of got out?' His voice is harder.

'No.'

'No I shouldn't of?'

'No I don't know.'

Jared sighs. Some of the women have brought thermos flasks and cups. They sip coffee, eat biscuits.

'Have a nice fucking picnic, ladies,' mutters Jared, and he turns and leaves the room, his footsteps turning down towards the bathroom. The door slams after him.

I've got time I reckon, if I'm quick.

Down the path I go, so nervous my toe snags twice on the cracks, even though I would know the depth and catch of them in my sleep. A little girl with red hair, a kid about four, sees me coming and tugs on her mother's T-shirt. They all turn and look at me then, and I swear it's like a bunch of old moos staring at me over the fence, giving me their full, doleful attention. Just before the letterbox I pull up.

'I'm not defending him,' I start, but my voice comes over wavery and thin. I clear my throat, start again. 'I'm on your side.'

Now the faces look disbelieving. Debbie's upper lip begins to lift into a sneer.

'Just give us a chance, eh?' But my voice has vanished again and they can't hear me. I feel suddenly exhausted, dry-mouthed after all the hours spent waiting for him to arrive, then sitting while he slept, and all the time smoking, smoking, smoking. I head back up the path and it's when I'm about halfway that they begin to yell out.

'You shouldn't have taken him back!' the first one bellows, and I'm pretty sure the voice belongs to Debbie.

'How're you going to stop him?' yells another.

'Murderers out!' yells another, and several voices join in: 'Murderers out! Murderers out! Murderers out!'

The first drops of rain fall as I reach the sagging porch and go inside. For a moment or two I listen to it drumming under their voices, thickening on the tin roof. In the kitchen at the end of the hall I can hear Jared moving about, opening and closing the fridge, the flick and hiss of a tear-tab.

I take a deep breath and go down to him, and as I do I can sense the women on the street begin to move away, not that I can hear them from here. They're doing the right thing: the rain is falling heavily now and I know as well as any mother does that you shouldn't leave your baby out in the weather. If you ever catch yourself at it, if you're doing it by mistake or on purpose, then you should face up to the fact that one day, eventually, you're going to have to make it up to him.

Nativity with Endymion

On a Friday evening, mid-December, Mona dragged herself in from shopping for her forty-fourth Christmas to find the local circular lying open on the table.

>CAN'T STAND CHRISTMAS?
>read the title, then:
>*Our team of qualified anaesthetists, weight specialists,*
>*psychiatrists and plastic surgeons await your*
>*Yuletide Time-out. Phone for an appointment.*
>*General Practitioner's recent full physical required.*
>>*AVOIDANCE THERAPY INC*
>>*Endymion Clinic*
>>*Remuera Road*

As luck would have it, Mona had seen her GP recently about a recurring sick-leave issue, so she made an appointment for 7.30

on Monday morning. During the phone call the receptionist had had to shout above the racket of power tools in the background.

'Oh yes, we're still very new,' she yelled. 'We only opened last week. See you on Monday.'

Instead of present-wrapping, Mona got on with her marking: the Year 10 Mathematics exam, which had to be finished and graded by Wednesday. The untidy numbers jumped before her eyes and it was difficult to concentrate; her mind kept wandering back to the little ad. Did it really mean what she thought it meant? No doubt it would be very expensive. How expensive? She could sell her car, if necessary. They'd still have Rod's car, she could always bus to work, thousands of people did, why couldn't she? Surely she could get the money together somehow . . .

She hardly slept that night or the night after, and continued her marking on Sunday while her teenage girls were off gallumphing their large and muscled bodies around at beach volleyball before they went with friends to watch videos and drink beer all afternoon. The day dragged by until her large and sunburnt husband came home from his weekend away fishing. While she fried up the catch he took a shower, coming out into the kitchen with a towel around him, his back and tubby tum as scarlet as Santa's suit. He matched the season.

Finally Monday dawned, with Mona up early and full of anticipation, curiosity and relief — a sunny, heady, fairy-tale blast: something she had longed for for years had come true and just in time. This year more than any other, Christmas just seemed too much, too hard, and it took too much of an effort to look into her heart and find out why. It didn't seem to be anything to do with commercialisation, or hollow rites, not as it had when she was younger. It was something else — something she couldn't identify: a sense of collapse, of seasonal disaffection, of wanting it to be early January already with it all over. Or was she just mean-spirited?

While the girls crashed around the kitchen, banging into each other and hooting as they packed their own lunches from an assortment of pre-packaged snacks, Mona called out, 'See you!' from the front door, and drove off.

The clinic was in a wealthy suburb where colonial money had built fine, tall, wooden houses in the nineteenth century. On the main road most had been demolished and replaced with new medical centres, clusters of surgeons wielding knives on every part of the human anatomy. Some of them advertised their area of speciality with an illustrated sign — a large foot, an ear, a breast. Mona hadn't been in this part of town for years. It had a strange kind of medical-carnival feel to it: the coloured words, the lights and shiny new buildings, the signs in all different languages.

ENDYMION CLINIC flashed one of the signs, and she slammed on her brakes without indicating — the car behind her stopping suddenly with a blast on its horn — and lurched down a right-of-way which used to be the driveway, Mona remembered, of a grand, gabled mansion with two turrets and wide verandahs upstairs and down. It was now entirely vanished away. At the front of the old property an orthopaedic clinic stood brand spanking new, though not as new as Endymion, which still had plumbers' and electricians' vans parked outside. The van she parked beside had sheets of glass angled against its sides like a beetle with its wings folded.

There was no one else in the woody waiting room, other than the receptionist and a woman with a small leather overnight bag set down at her feet. She looked rich: a blue tailored jacket, a silver-hued skirt made of fabric as lustrous as the pearls at her throat. As Mona sat down the woman glanced up at her and smiled.

'Come to have a look around?'

'That's right,' said Mona.

'Oh, you'll love it,' said the woman, closing her magazine. 'I made the first available appointment for treatment. They've got Powell, you know.'

'Powell?' She didn't remember the name from the ad.

'Face man. Famous. My birthday's the sixteenth of January, so I'll be around and about again for the Northern Hemisphere spring. Fifty years old, yes, that's true, but once again without a wrinkle, half a stone slimmer, gleaming top to toe from twice-daily massages and no memory of the ghastly anniversary. Wonderful, don't you think, dear?'

Mona nodded.

'Have you thought what music you'd like? You can choose your own — or foreign-language tapes . . . but I expect they'll tell you all about it.'

'I'm just here for Christmas,' said Mona, faintly.

The waiting room had begun to fill — several women of varying ages and two nervous-looking men.

A nurse came and led her away up one floor to a leafy atrium. They walked along an open-railed corridor that ran along a windowed exterior wall until they came to a row of rooms on the other side, with a different flower on each door. Mona was *Nasturtium*.

The nurse left her perched on the edge of the bed with the door ajar. After a few minutes a man in a dark business suit arrived.

'Benjamin France,' he said, shaking her hand. 'I'll just take up five minutes of your time to explain the legal situation.'

He ran through his twenty bullet-points, which could have been neatly summarised in only two: that there was no cover from medical insurance as this was revolutionary therapy, and that she was to sign an affidavit to the effect that she would not initiate litigation should the therapy fail or damage her. Leaving her with the form, he hurried off.

Through the gap in the door Mona watched nurses escort women and the occasional man. There were glimpses of doctors, too, passing with paperwork under their arms.

One came in to see her, with a name badge that simply read 'Anaesthetist'.

'You are?' he asked, taking the chair beside the bed.

'Here for Christmas,' she told him. He handed her a photograph.

'This is the Endymion Room,' he said, 'where you will be kept in a medically induced coma for your elected period of time.'

The picture showed a number of high, narrow beds with large plastic bubbles covering them. Beside each bed, inside each clear membrane, was a tall stand that held bottles and sprouted tubes. In a mural on the far wall a beautiful young man sprawled, fast asleep, with a glowing female form bending over him. Endymion, Mona supposed, from the legend. She peered more closely at the beds and noticed that some held pale bodies of varying shapes and sizes, all female, mostly on their backs, some on their fronts.

'The picture is, of course, posed,' said the anaesthetist. 'In the normal course of events the equipment would be in effect.'

'Pardon?' said Mona.

'The feeding and drainage tubes and monitors and so forth.'

'Oh.'

'Each individual bubble is kept at the temperature you prefer, and your weight is carefully graded and adjusted towards your preference. Do you have your letter from your GP?'

'It's being emailed through,' she told him.

'And have you had a general anaesthetic before? Any problems? Any questions?'

They went through his list and he hurried off, much like the lawyer had, and it was the same with the weight specialist — who talked about an intravenous mix of vitamins and minerals; the psychiatrist — who talked about the seriousness of Mona's decision and the possible implications of Christmas 2004 never featuring in her memory; and the plastic surgeon — who stood her in front of the mirror and hauled back her jowls.

There was even a physiotherapist who brought along a naked dummy. She lay it on the bed and demonstrated the exercises and massage Mona's body would enjoy while her absconded mind took its Yuletide vacation. A sound technician consulted her about the variety of music she would prefer to have ebbing into her comatose brain through earplugs.

'Or would you prefer a subliminal language?' he asked.

The last consultant was the accountant, who tallied her preferences at $30,879 for ten days with attention from Mr Powell, and $21,011 without it.

Mona's heart sank. Her car wasn't worth a quarter of the lowest quote.

Back in the carpark she noticed the time — 11.45 — and realised she'd completely forgotten she was supposed to be going in to work. How had she done that? Her mind must have been so completely taken up with longing to be one of the peaceful ones on the slabs.

On the motorway she put her foot down, heading out to her school, a large co-ed in the city's west. As she zipped along she was aware of only two words that kept rising in her mind, and they were Bank Loan. Why not? Other people borrowed to go to the Cooks, or Fiji, to lie in the sun. This was the same, but different.

Skewed across both lanes on the off-ramp was a truck, which Mona didn't see until it was too late. Her last observation, before she was knocked unconscious, was that the truck was laden with Christmas trees, a neat forest of horizontally stacked pines, now frothing over the edges of the tray and tumbling and flying around the car with the noise of thunder, shattering the windscreen.

She came around in a quiet, cool room and thought at first it was Endymion, but the faces staring down at her belonged to her husband and daughters, and she couldn't think why they would be here when she'd resolved to keep her whereabouts a secret. There was a variety of transparent tubes conveying liquid to and from her body.

Rod's face lit up at the dawning consciousness in her eyes. Above his red forehead drooped a Santa hat at a rakish angle. Her nostrils felt scoured, sensitive: there was a strong hoppy smell of meaty beer from him and something sweet and alcopop from the girls.

'Hello, darling,' he said. 'Welcome back.'

'Hi, Mum,' said the girls, and she thought they looked a little bewildered, sad even, as they hunched by the bed.

'It's Christmas Day, Mum,' said Jem, whose happy eyes were unaccustomedly teary.

Mona nodded. The tendons of Nic's strong hand closed around the loose strings of her own.

'You okay, Mum?' Nic was saying. 'You all there now?'

'Yes, dear,' said Mona, 'I think so.'

Three Times a Week

Within a month of arriving they'd bought a house. A love-nest, Renee called it, optimistically. It was a cottage of the type that abounded in the city's inner suburbs: fully renovated, around a century old, flat-fronted, its bull-nose verandah frilled with wooden lace. Renee planted a vigorous climbing rose and by the end of the summer it had wound a family of multi-labial heads around the plump knees of the verandah posts. The flowers were heavily scented, pale yellow. Renee had spent most of her time in the garden, composting, laying out lettuces, beans, tomatoes, and preparing in the tiny front yard a rich, dark, circular bed for the sapling she told him was a kowhai. It would have yellow flowers next spring, she said, around the time of her thirtieth birthday.

A year later, a week after the big party, while they stood side by side at the granite bench with its double sink, she showed him a picture of a kowhai bloom on her tea towel, a birthday gift from one of her little nieces. Her blonde head glowed yellow in the glass above the sink, the glass of the window that gave out onto their backyard, a scoop of dark before the lights of the neighbours' windows.

'See —' She held the cloth up and took hold of his arm. He felt her body press up against him, her breath on his cheek. Beneath the bubbles his fingers groped for the potscrub. 'Pretty, eh?'

She smelt of soap from her post-gardening soak, from the scene of her first disappointment of the day. When he'd taken her in a glass of wine she'd looked up at him with that teasing, playful glint in her eye, the soft smile below it. 'Thanks, honeybun,' she'd said, and reached out for him, her bubble-coated arm fluffy as a mink coat. He'd given her a tiny smile before hurrying out of the room.

Now he kept his fingers firmly underwater, a fleet of ten hot, fleshy submarines. Renee lifted her face and kissed him once on his jaw before stepping away to apply herself, energetically, to the forks. She was only showing affection, he told himself — she wouldn't approach him a second time in one day, not any more.

After the dishes they went through to the living room with its ratty furniture, all brown-shellacked wood inherited from Renee's aunt. Renee thought the chairs were antiques, but they rather reminded Alistair of the furniture at his Cambridge college — Downing, which was one of the poorest. He'd said as much to a guest at Renee's party, one of the girls from his office. Like him, she was in programming, but several rungs below him.

'I didn't know they had a university down there,' she said. 'There's so many of them now,' and he realised she meant the place south of Hamilton. Couldn't she hear his English accent?

Perhaps it was because Renee had returned home with one as well, though she had always been a rounded-vowel kind of girl. In New Zealand, she'd explained to him soon after they met, she was probably almost upper class. 'We have a class system too,' she'd said, almost defensively. 'We'd be up there somewhere, with my father's prominence, where we live, what we own, all our old money.'

While his wife reclined on the sofa, Alistair took an armchair and felt the cracks in the leather squabs push fine ridges into his thin summer shorts. Renee pointed the remote and brought up an English drama, all horsey women in pearls, and lay back, yawning, her head tilted on the pillow. Alistair took his eyes off her and let them wander over the varnished fireplace surround with its ugly mauve imitation-Victorian tiles.

'We love television because television is a world where television doesn't exist,' he said.

'Eh?' Renee had folded her hands over her tummy. They were tanned a milky brown, as smooth and shiny as her fine blue sweater. The pale blue and brown were matching hues.

'A quote — I read it somewhere. An American said it.'

'We don't have to have it on if you don't want it.' Renee's voice was soft. She hit the mute button.

On the mantelpiece was a pink cardboard hatbox full of pink and white flowers. When you looked into the hatbox from above, the pink flowers curved into two digits on a white background — 30. A blue and green photograph protruded to one side.

It wasn't a photograph, though. It was a card. His card. Which did have a photograph on the front: a salt-misted image of a wild, roaring beach, the white surf, the black sand, a helicopter shot. In the shop he'd thought it was potent, masculine.

'What's that doing out here?' He stood, picked it up. 'This is private.' He'd given it to her in the bedroom on the day, with an amber necklace and a cup of tea. Hadn't she sat it up on her bedside table after she'd hooked the beads around her throat? He'd thought it would stay there.

'I put all my cards up there before the party,' Renee was telling him. 'Don't worry. Your one was behind Mum's flowers. That's how come I missed it when I put the others away.'

That's how come, he thought irritably. Amazing that a girl with all her advantages had never made anything of her life. Then the breath caught in his throat. 'Did you say "before the party"?'

'Yes. Mmm.' She sounded a little anxious now. She was thinking it through.

'So anyone could've picked it up and read it?'

She said nothing, but she sat up, swung her legs around to face him. He took the photograph between thumb and forefinger and, as he did so, had a champagne-hazed recollection of James and Rachel and someone else looking at him strangely as he handed around a plate of food. They were standing by the mantelpiece. Had they read it?

'It was behind Mum's flowers,' Renee said again, as if the flowers were a magic talisman against the invasion of their privacy. He opened the card, read his own handwriting: *Dearest Ren, not just a birthday wish but a faithful promise to make love to you three times a week. Your loving husband, Bear.* There was no chance that any prying guest would have doubted the card's author because of his foolish inclusion of 'husband'. If only he'd just put 'Bear', her private name for him, a kind of rhyming endearment of Alistair, then the card's origins would've been blurred. They might've thought she was having an illicit affair, which would have been preferable. Good God. Was he really that kind of man? One who would prefer their friends suspected Renee of adultery than know his deadening truth?

He held the card and watched his wife, who turned her flushed face away from him. The amber beads glowed around her neck. The biggest bead, at the front, nestled into the bow of her throat, had an insect trapped in its ancient resin. As if she sensed him looking at it, Renee brought her hand to the bead, rolled it gently in her fingers. Her throat was one of her erogenous zones, she'd told him once — she liked him to lick and kiss her there. Perhaps the lolling bead was giving her pleasure. He couldn't help the way he was. If it was winter and they had lit the fire, he would have thrown the card into it.

Renee went to bed some time before him and when he followed she was asleep, the lights off, even though he'd made a point of slipping in while she was in the bathroom to turn on his bedside lamp.

He lay in the darkness, seething. She knew he could only get to sleep if he read first. Why had she turned it off? It would have been a small act of kindness on her part to have left it on. Monday tomorrow, he told himself. A rapid-fire early-morning coffee at the bench while he made himself an unappealing sandwich for lunch, pre-ordered by his overwhelming mortgage. No panini in a nearby café for him. Turning his head on the pillow to warm a suddenly chilled ear, he pictured himself shaving in the laundry, a small mirror propped on the tub taps, so that he didn't have to shave in the bathroom and wipe mist from the mirror while Ren chattered and showered beside him.

Perhaps I should get some help, he thought, pulling the sheets around his shoulders. Renee shifted from her side to her front, to sleep in that strange splayed way she had, one leg in hurdling position, the other ramrod straight, her head twisted.

God knows there were enough places advertising help. *Sex For Life*, read the ad in the *Herald*. There were shelves of books on sexual dysfunction in the health sections of bookshops, websites devoted to it, therapists who specialised in curing it. Three times a week, he'd promised her after the last bout of tears and rage.

'You're only thirty-four years old,' she'd sobbed. 'What's the matter with you? You make me feel dirty; you make me feel as if I'm a sex-fiend or a pervert or something.'

'I don't make you feel anything,' he'd said, then slammed off to the corner dairy to buy a packet of fags, which is what she'd made him do. The card, on her birthday a week later, was an attempt to mend things.

Now, another whole week had passed and he'd managed it — what, once? On Wednesday night. Afterwards Renee had murmured something and he'd asked her to repeat it. 'Thank you,' she'd said, in a small, sad voice, and he'd wanted to push her away in sudden rage. But he hadn't. He'd held her in his arms and wanted to cry. 'I'm just the way I am,' he'd said. There had only been two girlfriends before Renee and both associations were brief. Once he'd gone with a man who picked him up in a London bar but that had interested him even less. He felt nothing — neither pleasure nor revulsion. Eros didn't thrive in everyone, he believed; its absence was not necessarily due to past trauma or repression. To live without Eros was a way of being, painless and calm. A relationship complicated things. Just his luck, then, to have been born in an era where sexual prowess was prized above all else — and thanks to a new generation of drugs he wouldn't be safe from it, even when he was old and grey.

Renee turned to face him and slipped an arm around him, drew him close. 'Cold,' she murmured, and he thought she'd surfaced, that she'd want to talk, but after a moment her breath came again, regular and slow. Her encompassing arm, warm and soft around his ribs, gave a gentle squeeze, released, squeezed again. Why did she love him so much? he wondered. He should never have come to New Zealand, should never have let her talk him into the marriage of convenience so that she could extend her stay in London. The marriage had become just that. A marriage. Even in sleep her body was demonstrative.

He turned to face her and kissed her on the cheek. Perhaps they should have a baby. Perhaps that would help. His best mate in England had complained about how the nookie had dried up after the birth of his child. He pictured Renee holding a baby in her arms, a fuzz-headed, wobble-necked newborn. The image came to him as swiftly as if it were a memory, as if he'd already seen it in reality, like an icon of the Madonna. A child would solve a lot of problems; they were generally cuddly creatures. Renee could cuddle the child. He could make it happen, he could plant his own garden. He kissed her again, gently, until she stirred and woke.

In the morning, when he left, late, for work, with Ren singing behind him in the shower, he noticed that the little kowhai tree had blossomed. This year it was covered in heavy, pendulous trumpets in a deep, triumphant gold.

Drowned Sprat

'I'm just a gigolo for married women,' he told his fifth glass plaintively, and whichever of his old mates had bent their ear to him over the music. Had either of them? He looked around the table. There had been a boastful conversation earlier about literature — the sort of talk he usually enjoyed — but he hadn't partaken of it, had only half listened and wondered idly if Glen's contribution was dredged deep from Contemp. Poetry 101, or if he'd read any Pound in the twenty years since he graduated. Himself, he never went to university. He'd gone out as court reporter for a small-town rag, and learned fast about human nature at its most base, duplicitous and unintentionally amusing.

The duo, a silver-haired pianist and a big-voiced handsome woman, moved away to the bar to take a break.

'He was a fucking fascist, anyway,' Glen said now, out of the silence.

They hadn't heard him, then — they were still on the last topic.

'Everyone was a fascist then.' Tom leaned his narrow elbows in a slick of beer.

'Like who?'

'Like most of the middle class in the thirties. They had a taste for it. Fascist principles, anti-Semitism and all that shit.'

'Fascist principles,' repeated Glen. 'You're talking crap as usual. What do you know about fascism? Define it.' His plump, square fingers rolled a smoke.

The musician had gone back to the piano already, standing over it with a glass in his left hand. With the other, he picked out a riff that wasn't loud enough to drown out their talk, which was unfortunate, thought Maurice. He wanted to drift quietly around in his own head, take a placid, circuitous route to the dark house of inebriation. He went to the bar for another round.

The last woman had been prescient, he could see that now. 'You're taking revenge,' she'd said. She'd also said a lot of other things that had seemed more alarming at the time. 'I don't sleep with men I don't love.' 'Do you think I'm falling in love with you?' 'I wish I could stay.' 'Who are you avenging?'

He wanted to scream at her now for taking up room in his thoughts; he wanted to scream at her to fuck off out of his head. She was stopping him from getting properly drunk.

'Put it on my tab,' he said to the barman.

She would lie in his arms, flushed and only just still beautiful. She was at the tail-end of her beauty, he'd considered at the time — he'd just caught it. He'd seen photographs of her for years, pictures published in newspapers and magazines since her first major role, when she was still in her twenties. She'd played a troubled totty in a 1980s soap, not that he ever watched it. He'd followed her international career, though — it was difficult not to. She'd had a lot of media coverage for not much action. And here she was back in New Zealand, and in love with him. He considered she was making an error of judgement.

'You'd never look twice at me,' he said to her once. 'Someone like you — with someone like me.'

He put the glasses down: beer for himself and for Glen, juice for Tom, who was newly remarried and addressing his alcohol problem. Maurice had never thought that would happen. He felt abandoned to the alien twin causes of sobriety and domesticity. At the wedding reception Tom's teenage daughter had found him puking into the agapanthus that edged the carpark.

'I feel a bit sick too,' she told him, standing so close he could smell her perfume over the stench of his up-ended guts. Issey Miyake. The prescient one had worn that. You learned a lot about perfume from certain kinds of women: perfume was something — yet another something — women were territorial about. He'd made some mistakes in the past impressing different women with his scent recognition. They immediately wanted to know how he knew, how he did it.

Tom's daughter had rubbed his bony back while he wished she'd go away.

'Poor old Maurice,' she'd said. 'You've got so thin. When are you going to get married again? I've still got the pictures, you know, even though you're probably not supposed to, you know, keep pictures from marriages that didn't last — prob'ly bad luck . . .'

She'd prattled on for a while but he hadn't listened, his mind instead being taken up with an image of her in her role as flower-girl at his wedding eight years earlier, when she was still an innocent child, not this solicitous, yabbering young woman.

'How's Livvie?' he asked Tom suddenly, taking the third-to-last cigarette from his packet.

'Fine, I think. Haven't seen her for a while. She's been at her mother's.'

He'd said the daughter's name when he'd meant to say the new wife's, which was suddenly slipping away from him in a fog of beer and exhaustion. And hunger. When had he last eaten anything? He grabbed at Tom's wife's name half-heartedly. Did it begin with S?

Tom was looking at his watch and he hadn't touched his juice. Surely his mate wouldn't abandon him yet, leave him here with Glen when it was hours before he would want to go to bed, probably alone, unless he went further up Ponsonby Road to a bar that women frequented more than they did this one. Packs of single thirty-somethings lurked about SPQR, their children at home tucked up in bed, babysitters dozing in front of the TV. A miasma of desperation hung around them; every instinct warned him away from them. Why didn't more women go out drinking alone? he wondered. He pictured one now, conjured her onto a stool by the bar, long legs crossed, a wedding ring glinting on her finger. He gave her glossy black hair, heavily lidded eyes, a full mouth . . .

She wouldn't look twice at him, a woman like that. Not unless she'd watched his series, the one that went to air in the middle of last year: *Back Page*, a black and sexy drama set in a newspaper office. If she knew that *Back Page* was his baby, then she might be curious. People had imagined all sorts of things from the show — they'd imagined him to be warm, romantic, funny, searingly intelligent.

Tom was standing, shrugging on his jacket.

'See ya, mate,' he was saying. 'Got to pick Shona up.'

And he was gone, passing under the cut-out faux clouds in the high blue ceiling, down the soggy-carpeted stairs to the lit mall below. Glen pursed his fat lips and blew through them in that infuriating way he had. He waggled his eyebrows and Maurice managed to expose his teeth in a rictus of a smile. He had no idea what Glen meant — he supposed he was implying some kind of solidarity. There they were, two single, early-middle-aged guys, 7.07 pm on a spring Friday and nowhere to go.

'Just off for a slash,' said Glen, and he got up, pushing his belly ahead of him through the men at the bar.

He'd walk down to the water. He'd walk down to the tank farm. He lit up his second-to-last fag and got out of there before Glen came back.

Halfway down College Hill his legs threatened to give out under him, his knees like jelly. What he'd thought at first was his own clammy sweat sitting like a row of dead frogs on his brow turned out to be the beginning of rain, a fine mist of it barely visible in the headlights of passing cars. He shivered in his light jacket, stuck his fag in his mouth to free his hands to tuck in his T-shirt.

'Gigolo,' said his uneven footsteps on the steep path. 'Gi go lo, gi go lo, gi go lo.'

He dodged the traffic across Victoria Street into the darkening park. He'd told the actress he wouldn't do it again — he would indulge in intellectual pursuits, keep to himself. That was after she'd told him that her husband had found out, that he'd left her, that her two children were bereft. She'd probably expected him to say something else, something more sympathetic. Did she expect him to take the blame for what had happened? Why should he? He'd been honest, relatively, from the start. I'm in love with someone else, he'd told her, with another married woman who wouldn't leave her husband. I'm still in love with her. I will always be in love with her.

At first she hadn't minded. She'd even laughed when he told her his heart was a drowned sprat. She'd enjoyed the metaphor. Then she began to talk about reviving it, hauling it up from its murky depths and exposing it to the air. She said it was easy to love, that she loved lots of people, that there was no big mystery, that it wasn't the rare thing he thought it was. She gave him a bad case of the bends.

On the other side of the park he had to wait to get across Fanshawe Street, which was clogged with traffic waiting to get onto the Harbour Bridge. He shifted from one foot to the other like a jogger, while the wind that swirled around the concrete columns of the flyover cut into his ribs and flung icy drops of water into the back of his neck. It was an arctic spring, even this far north. Maybe he should go away for a while — just for a few days — go somewhere in the South Pacific and warm his bones on a white-hot beach; be waited on by large, kind, brown women, from whom he'd be safe. They wouldn't fancy him — he was too narrow and bloodless. He would pursue intellectual matters flat on his back, or possibly with another small tourist who happened to be in the same resort and happy to play.

The lights had changed and he'd nearly missed his crossing; he sprinted across the road, his stomach roiling. A nautical-themed restaurant flung misshapen portholes of light across the path. Inside, a waiter in a striped shirt bent to a table of early diners, holding a match to a candle.

Past the chandlers, offices and dinghy shops he went, towards the gleaming tanks at the point. At the end of the row of low-rise buildings the night opened up around him into yards and truck bays and a smell of fish and salt and engine oil forced into his chest like an embolism. He slowed down and breathed deeply through his mouth, the cold air making his teeth ache. The rain had eased off; there were a few stars. He thought perhaps the temperature had dropped; it grew colder with every step towards the water.

He was among the tanks on the point now; they lifted into the dark — cool monoliths of white, ladders curled at their sides. There was one car parked at the safety railing by the sea, its windows steamed up. For a moment he imagined knocking on its window, just so he could see their faces. He wanted to see love in their faces; it would still be there when they turned away from each other perhaps, if he surprised them before they sensed he was there. Was it love, going on in the car? Maybe it was just a transaction, a simple exercise in getting it rocking gently, as it was, on its springs.

He put his back to it, leaned over the railing and looked into the water, pressing his empty stomach into the rough wood. When he was younger, and he got like this — what was it, depressed? — he'd think about suicide: chucking himself off bridges, filling himself with pills, taking a sweet slide to oblivion. Now he knew where the barrier was and he hid behind it; he didn't let those thoughts progress. That was middle age: a knowledge that every day would be pretty much the same, a preparedness for that.

He heaved a sigh, hoisted himself over the white bars and sat down on the narrow stone ledge above the tide. Traffic roared on the Harbour Bridge high on his left, louder on the westerly wind, and the soles of his scummy shoes skimmed choppy waves. He brought his knees up, hugged them close. It was true, what he'd told the actress and a few others besides. He was still in love with the other woman; he needed to be. It afforded him a fecund melancholy that fuelled him through life and in and out of endless liaisons with other men's women; it enabled him to preserve his solitude and keep at bay a crippling guilt about the failure of his own marriage. If the sprat-drowner changed her mind and wanted him back, he'd reject her. That was a given, a certainty.

A party yacht motored by, sails furled, lifting and falling in the chop. The cabin lights showed silhouettes of men and women sheltering from the weather. Only one couple stood on the deck, wrapped around each other, their faces joined. God, they were behind him and in front of him: there was no escape from people wanting attachment. The car was really rocking now — he could hear it creaking, but kept his face averted. There might be a naked arm flung up, the sole of a foot pressed against the windscreen: whatever, he wouldn't be witness to it. Who were they anyway — teenagers, adulterers, the affianced? He hoped they would live to regret it.

He put the last cigarette in his gob, screwed up the packet and chucked it into the water. It bobbed around, a small luminescent square, the frill of silver gleaming in the street-light. He watched it for a few moments, while he tried to light up. It vanished in the same instant he decided the flame would only catch if he stood and put his back to the wind.

The car was quite still and one of its doors was opening. A tousled young man was climbing out, straightening his shirt, buttoning his trousers. He and Maurice each pretended the other didn't exist, though Maurice passed close by him to begin his homeward walk. As he drew level, the man leaned into the car and said something to the lover inside. It was a man's voice that answered.

'You're beautiful, you know that, Mr Collins?'

Two blokes, then. The man leaning into the car had a gold band on his wedding finger.

Highly Combustible read a sign on the wire fence on the next block. *Danger. No Naked Flames. No Entry.*

Maurice sucked hard on his smoke, tipped his head to the top of the tallest tower where a single star punctured the sky for a moment before it was obliterated by a scudding cloud, itself invisible against the dark.

The woman who stayed with her husband, the woman he loved, told him: *You gave us what we needed, you gave us a spark.*

A spark.

He'd give them spark.

While he looked around for a stone he sucked hard on what was left of his cigarette, careful to leave a centimetre or so still to burn. From his pocket he took a hair elastic, a tragically preserved trophy from the heartbreaker who'd always tied her hair back before they made love, as if she was cooking and not wanting to shed into the soup. It stretched around the stone twice, securing the cigarette, and then it was only a case of lobbing it as high and far as he could, over the fence. Before he turned to leave, he waited to hear it land and it seemed to him the click of stone on concrete came from high above his head, from the top of the middle-sized tank.

The nautical restaurant was full, the traffic was thin, the park oozed danger and the gradient of College Hill threatened to rise up and smack him in the face. His breath rasped in his chest; he had the strangest sensation that the pores in his back had opened, ready for the boom, which he knew would never come. The tethered cigarette, his tiny bomb, would have been extinguished by the rain, which was now falling thick and fast, obscuring even the other side of the road. Outside what used to be the Gluepot he waited for a cab, drenched and shivering. When he got home, he decided, he would finish the half bottle of Jim Beam he'd hidden from himself in a cupboard. He would not answer the phone, he would take a new packet of fags from the carton, he would lie on his sofa and sleep.